D1452061

SECRETARY
OF THE CITY

LEE NAVLEN

Secretary of the City

©Lee Navlen

Print ISBN 979-8-35092-204-2

eBook ISBN 979-8-35092-205-9

Aired March 9, 2023 - 9:00 AM ET

THIS IS A RUSH RADIO TRANSCRIPT. THIS COPY MAY NOT BE IN ITS FINAL FORM AND MAY BE UPDATED.

[9:00:00]

BOB LEMOULLEC, 1010 WINS NEWS ANCHOR: It's Wednesday, March 9th, 2023, I'm Bob LeMoullec and here's what's happening. New York Governor Simon Miller for president? That's the rumor coming out of Albany, but the governor? Well, earlier this morning, he wasn't saying much.

(SOUNDBITES)

GOV MILLER: My focus remains the people of New York. I have served this great state now for six years and it's the best job I've ever had. I'll leave it at that.

REPORTER: So, we can forget the White House?

GOV MILLER: Let's just say, if things change, you'll be the first to know.

BOB LEMOULLEC, 1010 WINS NEWS ANCHOR: Not exactly a denial, but not a confirmation either. The democratic governor, who will be 74 in May, is polling well nationally but for now, mum seems to be the word. We do have some breaking news. There's been a small plane crash in Rahway, New Jersey. Our own 1010 WINS NEWS reporter, Mike Rowe, is on the scene. What's the latest Mike?

MIKE ROWE, 1010 WINS NEWS REPORTER: Yeah, Hey Bob, one victim, was taken to a local hospital. His injuries are being called critical. The single engine aircraft was attempting to make an emergency landing on a baseball field, not far from Linden Airport. By the looks of it, the plane hit the ground hard. There is smoke but local rescue crews have put out the fire. Of note, there are witnesses saying a woman was seen dragging the injured man from the airplane. She then, and again this is according to a few witnesses, jumped into a taxi and left.

BOB LEMOULLEC, 1010 WINS NEWS ANCHOR: A woman left the scene? Was she on the aircraft?

MIKE ROWE, 1010 WINS NEWS REPORTER: Yes, it looks that way.

BOB LEMOULLEC, 1010 WINS NEWS ANCHOR: OK, That's Mike Rowe, reporting live from Rahway, New Jersey. So, again, at least one person was injured following the crash of a single engine airplane not far from Linden Airport. Unconfirmed reports indicate that a woman helped the critically injured victim before leaving the scene. As we get more details, we will share them with you.

CHAPTER 1

Thursday, March 9th, 2023
10:00 AM
From: The Desk of Liz White

It was Henry's wife calling. A very busy woman but she didn't actually work, she didn't have to. Leighton Jones was Park Avenue, a true Manhattan socialite. America's 0.001 percent. Leighton grew up privileged and married into even more privilege when she wed my boss, Henry Jones.

"Hello Leighton."

"Umm, Liz, I'm in Rahway."

I wasn't sure what she meant.

"Rahway?"

"Yeah, I need Richie. Where is Richie?"

Richie was Leighton and Henry's driver but I didn't know where he was.

"Leighton, perhaps he's parked outside the townhouse?" I said trying to at least cover for Richie whose most important responsibility was being available for all of Leighton's needs, usually in or around her six story Upper East Side home.

"Well, I need him! Call him immediately and tell him I'm in Rahway and to..."

The call dropped. I hung up confused, where was Leighton and what was this Rahway thing about? I called Richie, maybe he knew something. He picked up without saying hello.

"Hey Liz, you hear the radio?"

I assumed that meant there was some big sporting news thingy going on so I tried cutting him off but he kept talking.

"They're saying a small plane crash, and uhh, Mrs. J, she was on a small plane."

This made no sense to me. Why would Leighton Jones be on a small plane?

"Richie, what the hell are you talking about?" Between Leighton and Richie, no one was making sense.

"Liz, I'm sworn to secrecy, Mr. J can never know what I told you."

"Told me what, Richie?"

"Mrs. J, she's, I can't say."

"Well, Leighton just called me from Rahway, I think? Call her cell now!"

"She called you? When?"

"Just now, go call her! She's looking for you!"

"Thank Jesus! Just don't tell anyone what I told you." He said before hanging up.

I googled "small plane crash in Rahway" but nothing came up. Was Leighton in a plane crash? Nah, Richie was talking nonsense again, I was sure. I tried calling Leighton back but it went to voicemail, I tried a second and third time. On the fourth, she finally picked up.

"Leighton? Has Richie gotten in touch with you?"

"Oh, yes, he has." Leighton indicated as if everything were fine.

Relieved, I asked her if there was anything else she needed from me.

"Don't mention any of this to Henry." Leighton said before abruptly hanging up.

Any of what??

AIRED MARCH 9, 2023 – 11:00 AM ET

THIS IS A RUSH RADIO TRANSCRIPT. THIS COPY MAY NOT BE IN ITS FINAL FORM AND MAY BE UPDATED.

[11:00:00]

BOB LEMOULLEC, 1010 WINS NEWS ANCHOR: It's 11 AM in New York City, I'm Bob LeMoullec, and here's what's happening. A small plane crash in Rahway, New Jersey has turned into a bit of a mystery. The pilot has been identified as Christopher Crimi, an Italian national, and the famed chef and founder of The Italian Plate restaurant chain. He apparently departed from Teterboro Airport when he attempted to make an emergency landing. Officials say Crimi is in critical condition at an area hospital. Now here's the mystery. According to reports, a woman was seen helping the pilot to safety before leaving the scene of the crash. Our own 1010 WINS NEWS reporter, Mike Rowe is in Rahway, New Jersey and he's with some eyewitnesses. Mike?

MIKE ROWE, 1010 WINS NEWS REPORTER: Yeah, Hi Bob, it's a strange one for sure. I've spoken with some neighbors and they all are saying the same thing. They heard the crash and saw the smoking wreckage of the single engine aircraft shortly before the mystery woman climbed out. Tell me, sir, what did you see?

WITNESS #1: The plane went down hard. I saw smoke and fire, then a door opens and this woman dragged a guy from the plane before running away from the scene. I seen

4

a cab coming, she jumped in and off she went. I couldn't believe it!"

MIKE ROWE, 1010 WINS NEWS REPORTER: And you ma'am, you said she was dressed fashionably?

WITNESS #2: Yeah, a woman, a white woman, a brunette, I saw her running with her big fancy bag and fancy shoes. She just took off like she had somewhere else she needed to be.

MIKE ROWE, 1010 WINS NEWS REPORTER: So again, here's what we're learning at the scene. A woman was seen climbing out of the aircraft, holding what appeared to be some type of large handbag. She helped the pilot to safety before making a run for it. She hailed a passing taxi, climbed in and drove off. I have reached out to the local taxi company but they're not saying much at this hour.

BOB LEMOULLEC, 1010 WINS NEWS ANCHOR: Thank you, Mike Rowe for that report. Again, repeating our top story, one injured, the pilot, identified as Christopher Crimi, the founder of The Italian Plate restaurant chain and one woman apparently AWOL after a small plane crash in Rahway, New Jersey. That's it for me this morning. I'm Bob LeMoullec, 1010 WINS NEWS!"

CHAPTER 2

Thursday, March 9th, 2023

11:30AM

From: The Desk of Liz White

Leighton called again, demanding that I find Richie. I suggested she call him direct, to which she hung up on me. This was the part of the job that made me nuts. Yes, I was Henry Jones' secretary but I was also Leighton's de facto personal assistant and her middleman. She called on me to do everything for her from booking a flight to booking a hotel reservation to booking a restaurant reservation to booking an appointment with Frederic, her hairdresser to even finding her "magic mushrooms" when she decided for some reason that she wanted to see the "Dave Matthew Band".

"It's Matthews, not Matthew, Leighton."

"Oh, that's fine, do find those mushrooms, I've heard great things!"

Leighton would call me at the office from her bedroom to have the housekeeper, three floors below, bring her a cup of tea, or lunch. Per her "request", I've completed school projects for her twins. I've even made cheat sheets for the brats. Leighton has called from the back of the car, more than once, to find out why Richie, her driver, had her sitting in traffic. I've been forced to con doctors' offices for prescriptions for all of Leighton's various phantom medical conditions. It was like she only had one number stored in her phone, mine. Leighton would call at all hours too, often well past midnight. "It's late Leighton, what do you need?"

"It's late? It's only 11 PM." was perhaps her most annoying call since she was in San Francisco and I was in New York.

She was difficult but at the very least she was consistently where she was supposed to be, basically where I sent her. So, this plane crash thing and her being in Rahway, which according to the internet was a town in central New Jersey with a state prison, made no sense.

With this Leighton/plane mystery going on, Henry was holed up as usual inside his wall of glass office on the 55th floor with the brilliant, sweeping views of Midtown Manhattan. From my desk a few feet away, my view was Henry watching the cable business channel, CNBC and reading *The Wall Street Journal*. He motioned me in.

"Liz, did you see the news? You know Christopher Crimi, Leighton's old friend?"

I knew of Christopher. Leighton met him years ago, before my time, when she was fresh out of Penn State Law and decided to drop everything to move to Italy and become an international chef. Hilarious because in my 20 years with the Jones family, Leighton never once prepared a meal. That's what Bevy, the family cook and head- housekeeper, did. Christopher, on the other hand, became huge, launching The Italian Plate, an international chain of restaurants.

Henry continued, "Well, the news is saying he was in a small plane crash, it just came up on CNBC."

I was about to tell Henry what I knew of Leighton's involvement, but then I remembered Richie's warning not to say a word, so I didn't.

"They say Chris is in critical condition, maybe you can alert Leighton, she'll want to send flowers," Henry said, turning his attention back to his newspaper.

CHAPTER 3

Thursday, March 9th, 2023
12:00 PM
From: The Desk of Liz White

I knew that Leighton and Christopher kept in touch over the years via her email which I had access to. I actually had access to both Leighton and Henry's email accounts since I needed them in order to complete the multitude of tasks, I was presented with from both of them. They didn't know I did this but, since I was the one who originally set up their Gmail accounts nearly two decades earlier, I spied on both of them to my great benefit. While there was a strategy behind my unhindered access to the emails, I also often perused Leighton's "classic" sent emails for pure entertainment value. Some of my all-time favorites:

> Leighton to Henry
>
> Sent 2/16/07 @ 9:01 AM
>
> Henry, I think Liz is stealing. She was in my room and now it's missing. Please advise course of action xo.
>
> Leighton to Henry

Sent 4/15/18 @ 3:30 AM

Henry, I hate Liz. FIRE her and HIRE a MONKEY! xo

Leighton to Liz & Henry

Sent 5/11/17 @ 2:02 AM

Bevy stole my Ambien. She's sound asleep but I'm wide AWAKe! Find me an honest person WHO IS NOT A DRUG WHORE!

Scanning her current emails, I saw nothing between Leighton and Christopher but Leighton had also recently discovered text messaging, some 25 years after its invention, so perhaps that's how they were communicating.

I dialed Richie again.

"Richie, is it all good with Leighton?"

"Yeah, and no."

"What the hell does that mean, Richie? This is getting real fucked up!" I said despite being the type of person who rarely swore.

"Liz, it's like this and please, you didn't hear it from me, OK?"

"OK, Christ, tell me already!"

"Mrs. J has been playing pattycake with some rich prick, she gets on his little fucking tinker toy plane, he crashes the thing but she wasn't hurt."

"Well, that's great!" I shouted.

"Yeah, and no. Yeah, she says she's ok, but she doesn't want nobody to know she was ever on the plane, that's why she ran. Mr. J. can never know!"

My head was spinning.

"Where is she now?"

"She's at a train station in Rahway, waiting for me to come get her but there's all this traffic from I guess the plane crash."

"Please, let me know once you have her!"

"Don't say nothing to Mr. ..."

"I won't!"

I hung up the phone loud enough that Henry looked up at me and frowned.

CHAPTER 4

March 9th, 2023
1:00 PM
From: The Desk of Liz White

So, apparently, Leighton was on the plane with her old flame when it went down. She managed to not only get off the smoldering aircraft but she also found a taxi. But why was she taken to a train station? At the very least she would have demanded the driver return her to Manhattan. As I was trying to make heads and tails of the situation, Leighton called.

"Liz, Have Bevy run me a bath, I should be home in … Richie, when am I going to be home?"

In the background I heard Richie say, "maybe two hours."

"Two hours, ugh? You know what Liz, tell Bevy to hold off, I'll call you when we're closer."

Leighton was about to hang up when I shouted.

"Wait, Leighton!"

"Yes, Liz, what is it?" Leighton asked, sounding annoyed.

"Leighton, I'm just going to say it! There's been a plane crash, Henry saw it on the news. It was Christopher Crimi's plane, he was apparently flying it."

Leighton was silent for a moment.

"Liz, we must send flowers, have the card say this:

"Wishing you well." Leighton and Henry Jones"

Leighton hung up.

Wishing you well? That was all she wanted the card to say? I interrupted Henry who was on the floor doing his back stretches.

"Leighton would like me to send flowers. Has the news mentioned what hospital Christopher was taken to?"

"I don't think so." he said between grunts and moans. "What does she want the card to say?"

"Wishing you well."

"That's it? Henry asked as he reached out for my hands to help him up. "That's not enough. Have the card say this. Chris, we sure are glad we never accepted the offer to fly with you! Hope you recover soon. See you on the links – L & H."

Henry smiled as he slowly sat down at his desk, still breathing heavily from his exercises.

"OK, get working on those flowers. Oh, Liz, did she say what kind of flowers?"

"No."

"Maybe perennials. Or roses." Henry recommended.

"I'll send a nice arrangement if I can figure out where he is." I said cutting Henry off before he could make further suggestions.

"OK, just run it by Leighton first. Poor Chris, I warned him not to fly on his own. Since Thurman Munson, it's never been a good idea. Thurman Munson was my favorite player when I was a kid, boy, when he died..."

"Henry, you've told me about Herman Munster before."

"It's Thurman, oh you know what, never mind, it was a long time ago."

In truth, I knew it was Thurman Munson, not Herman Munster. In my 20 years with Henry, he's mentioned that name too many times to count but that's Henry. He'll tell you the same stories dozens of times, but he's the boss so sometimes you just had to take it; but if I had a way to cut the conversation short, I'd go for it.

As I was about to leave his office, CNBC broke in with an update on the crash.

Anchor: "We're learning details regarding a small crash involving Christopher Crimi, the CEO of The Italian Plate chain of restaurants. According to reports, he was piloting the plane when it went down in New Jersey. He's been rushed to an area hospital in critical condition. Of note, witnesses say a woman was on board too but somehow managed to leave the scene before rescue crews arrived. Her identity remains a mystery at this hour."

Henry looked at me and smiled.

CHAPTER 5

March 9th, 2023
3:00 PM
From: The Desk of Liz White

The story hit the newswires and was soon all over the internet. The top story was shifting from plane crash/CEO in critical condition to missing passenger who seemed to have saved, and then abandoned, the pilot moments after the plane hit the ground. At least I was able to find out which hospital Christopher had been taken to. The card included Leighton's wording, not Henry's.

Leighton called me back once Richie reached the Lincoln Tunnel to ask, or actually to tell me, to have her bath ready along with a bottle of Veuve Clicquot.

"It's been a day," as she put it.

I needed details but she was clearly in Leighton mode which meant she asked the questions, gave the orders and dictated where the conversation was going. Still, I tried to coax out of her what I could.

"Leighton, I sent the flowers. By the way, Christopher has been taken to a RWJ Hospital in Rahway."

"Oh my, that sounds like an awful place! Perhaps we can have him airlifted to New York Presbyterian instead? Do ask Henry."

Henry was on the board of directors at NYP, so perhaps he could, but I got the feeling it wasn't something he would be in a hurry to do.

"Leighton, I have to ask, why were you in New Jersey?"

"Shopping." was all she said.

"Well, is there anything else I should know?"

"No, just have the bath ready."

"OK." I said but just as I was about to hang up, Leighton called out my name.

"Yes, Leighton?"

"Henry doesn't know I shop in New Jersey, let's keep that quiet."

As she spoke, I was looking through the glass into Henry's office. He was on the phone laughing, holding a large unlit cigar and smelling it.

After hanging up with Leighton, I quietly picked up Henry's line and listened in, something I did often enough to pass the time. As usual, he was speaking with his best friend, Adam. The two were like chicks on the phone spending hour upon hour gossiping. Henry was saying.

"Yeah, they said some woman was seen running from the crash. Probably a girlfriend. He probably told her to get lost before his wife found out. I would!"

Adam interjected.

"How do you know this guy again?"

"Leighton does, they went to cooking school together years ago."

"I didn't know Leighton cooked!"

"Neither does Leighton!" Henry said laughing.

I nearly laughed too.

CHAPTER 6

Thursday, March 9th, 2023
3:30 PM
From: The Desk of Liz White

I knew Leighton had just survived a plane crash, one that nearly killed the pilot but she was already in stealth mode, not wanting Henry or anyone for that matter to know the truth. She was flying with her one time and perhaps current lover, a romance she kept so secretive that not even I knew about it.

Henry knew they were "friends" but I don't think he cared for Christopher in what I guess was a Henry sort of way. He would never slam or threaten someone but if he had issue with them, he just wouldn't be very warm. I knew that feeling, Henry was never that warm with me either.

I originally met Henry during my job interview on September 11th, 2001, yeah that day. I had just sat down in his midtown office with floor to ceiling windows that actually frightened me a little. As he was poring over my resume that included one prior 18-month secretarial job, there was a breaking news report on his TV, an airplane had hit one of the twin towers. To me the video made it clear it was a large plane but Henry insisted it was a small one.

"It's easy for these pilots to get confused. They'll put the fire out soon."

He continued interviewing me as the TV flashed live shots of the smoking building. He was pleased to learn that I was a fellow Episcopalian and that like Henry, my father had attended Harvard.

"How come you want to be a secretary?" He asked, believing that maybe due to our shared White Anglo-Saxon Protestant heritage I could be striving for more.

I told him the truth; I would be his secretary until I married.

"When will that be?"

"After I find a boyfriend."

Henry liked the answer. The second plane hit, it was obviously a terrorist attack. My only thought was, could other planes be out there looking for more sky scrapers to strike, like the one I was sitting in?

"Should we evacuate?" I asked Henry.

"I don't think that's going to be necessary." he said mere seconds before an alarm sounded, a voice over an intercom advising us to leave the building in an orderly fashion. We were further told to use the stairwell.

Henry wanted to take some work home with him so I helped him carry his briefcases down the 55 flights as he continued asking me various questions.

"What's your greatest strength?"

"It's my ability to think on my feet." I said as I juggled his stuff along with mine.

"And your greatest weakness?"

"I guess, skyscrapers."

Henry frowned.

Somewhere around the 15th story or so he asked me my salary requirements. He seemed surprised that I was asking for so much. Once we reached the street he shook my hand, thanked me for coming in and told me to follow up with him in a week or two. Before parting ways, he gave me his business card.

A week later I got the job but for $3,000 less than I wanted. I started one week after that and soon met Leighton. I never did find that boyfriend.

CHAPTER 7

Bevy called. She and I looked out for each other. As the Jones' family head housekeeper and cook, she saw their domestic life up close and I saw just about everything else. We relied on each other for information, for guidance, for gossip and most importantly for sanity. Knowing that her Romanian accent was thick, Bevy always made an effort to speak slowly and clearly.

"Mrs. J, she crash in plane. She crazy. She said not to tell no one but I tell you. She said plane go down, she thought she would die. Her friend knocked head hard, she pull him from plane but she was fine. She say she ran for her life, saw a taxi and get in."

"Bevy, she just left?

"Mrs. J says she not doctor, nothing she could do. She no want Mr. J to know, so she just leave."

"Bevy, did she look injured?"

Bevy laughed.

"Her hair was a mess, her shoe was broken, small cut on her knee but she still looked the same, annoyed."

I found myself laughing too.

"Bevy, how much champagne did Mrs. Jones drink when she got home?"

"Oh, she drink some of bottle. Told me to drink rest."

"Did you?"

"Oh, yes, bottle cost $200.00! I finish, got drunk, but I didn't like it."

CHAPTER 8

Thursday, March 9th, 2023
7:00 PM
From: The Desk of Liz White

Back at my apartment after quite the day, the news was focused on the missing passenger story. Authorities were hoping cameras at Rahway State Prison, not far from the crash site, picked up something so they were investigating that.

The second biggest story of the evening was Leighton's father, New York Governor Simon Miller, who was considering a run at the White House. I knew Governor Miller, a nice guy, he never forgot a birthday including mine so he had my vote but I was worried. Could Leighton's great escape hurt him? I imagined it might but what could I do?

I thought about calling my dad but he hated stories related to Leighton and Henry. Like Henry, he felt I should have strived for better. He had encouraged me to go to law school after college but truthfully, I was done with school. Four years of smoking pot and drinking got me a useless psychology degree. That was the extent of my educational experience and that was enough for me.

I did like typing and organizing and I wanted to live in New York City so at the age of 22, I packed up and left the North Shore of Massachusetts in search of a secretarial position. I quickly landed at an upstart advertising agency called Lobue & Lombardo. The partners, Tim and Jim were fairly young guys branching away from McCann Erickson to start their own place. Quickly, and with my help, they failed miserably. After 18 months, the three of us were unemployed. If not for the fact that we were going under, I likely would have been fired. Through the grapevine, I learned that some 20 years later, the two of them still blame me for the demise of Lobue and Lombardo but I don't see it that way.

They were bright enough guys but they weren't cut out to be bosses. Tim liked motorcycles but he was clumsy and had at least three accidents in the firm's 18 months of existence. He broke a leg once, an arm the other time and then there was a concussion. As the "Art Director," being unable to stand or draw or think clearly cost the agency more than a few clients as Tim didn't meet the deadlines. Jim was a lazy guy; he grew up somewhat rich and married a successful woman. He didn't believe he had to work hard. Instead, he found excuses. He had a cold, his kid had a cold, his wife wanted to go on vacation. He never worried about not getting work done.

There was also the silent partner, the guy with the real money, JK Stern who was very energetic and tough as nails. He quit high school and by 25 had become a well-known guy in the advertising business. JK didn't work out of our office but he stopped by often enough. Unbeknownst to Tim and Jim, he'd also secretly pick me up outside the building in his stretch limo so we could spin the city snorting cocaine as I gave him dirt on his partners. That was the thing with coke, it made me run my mouth and I think JK realized this. In short, nothing anyone did there worked but soon after that disaster, through a recruiter, I met Henry.

CHAPTER 9

Friday, March 10, 2023
7:00 AM
From: The Desk of Liz White

New York Post headline:

She Saved the Bag!

Turns out the *New York Post*, not the authorities, found the video. A camera from the state prison caught the plane hitting the ground hard along with footage of a tall brunette climbing out wearing Christian Louboutin red sole pumps. Quickly she pulled a man from the smoking wreckage before retrieving a Hermes Birkin, a handbag valued at over six figures. There could be no doubt, it was Leighton.

I wasn't sure what I was walking into as I took the elevator up to 55. Henry was already in his office watching CNBC and of course reading *The Wall Street Journal*.

"Liz, coffee please."

Well, that was very normal, nothing out of the ordinary there. I went to the kitchen and got his mug.

"So, Henry," I said, placing his coffee on his desk. "What's the latest with Christopher?"

Henry told me to close his door even though no one else worked in the office space.

"Liz, did I ever have you sign an NDA?"

"A non-disclosure agreement?" I asked.

Henry exhaled, he often found me quite frustrating.

"Yes, Liz, an agreement that essentially prohibits you from discussing what we do here."

Was Henry kidding? What we did was essentially invest his vast fortune. He also sat on various philanthropic boards but nothing he did was illegal. Henry was at his core a boy scout who just happened to be worth about one billion dollars. For those who say the rich are all crooks, it's not true, Henry was proof of that. Cheap maybe, especially when it came to paying me, but dishonest? No, not ever.

"Henry, you never had me sign anything like that but I assure you, everything I do for you stays confidential."

I assumed he was going to pivot and talk about the crash; Leighton surely must have told him.

"Great news and thanks for your discretion!" Instead, was all he said.

He tried dismissing me but I wasn't sure what he was talking about. Discretion regarding what? The crash, or was it something else?

"Henry, is there something specific we're talking about right now?"

"Specific, like what?"

"Why are you so concerned with my discretion right now?"

"No reason, hey how about another cup of your very delicious coffee!"

I grabbed his empty coffee mug from his desk.

"Hey Liz, did you see The *NY Post* headline?"

"I did."

"I wonder who the woman is!" he said smiling.

He knew nothing.

CHAPTER 10

Friday, March 10th, 2023
8:00 AM
From: The Desk of Liz White

Back at my desk, the phone rang, it was Leighton.

"Liz," she began. With Leighton there was never a hello or a good morning.

"I'll need you to do me a favor and please don't tell Henry."

It wasn't uncommon for Leighton to give me an order with additional instructions not to tell Henry. It made my job extremely difficult since I was basically a pawn in their game of hide the truth. At times Henry asked the same thing of me but it was much more common with Leighton.

"Please transfer, oh let's say $100,000 to my personal checking account, can you do that today?"

Leighton had a "spending problem". To Henry, it was no different than a gambling or drinking problem. If she had money, she spent it and she spent it all so Henry attempted to limit her cash to say no more than $50,000 a month to combat her "disease." It usually didn't work though because if she needed more money, she would come to me. The few times I tried bringing it up with Henry, he cut me off saying he didn't want to know, or better yet he didn't need to know what Leighton was up to. Frustrating yes, but it was their money so I did my best to follow orders and keep my mouth shut. But, $100,000? That would take some creativity on my part. I could borrow from a trust, or perhaps from some cash on hand elsewhere, just as long as Henry was kept in the dark until I could replace it. To summarize, yes, thanks to Leighton, I spent hours unable to sleep at night trying to figure out a way to borrow from Peter to pay Paul, or better yet to borrow from Henry to pay Henry.

"I can move cash into your Citibank account, Leighton."

"Oh, wonderful! Well in that case make it $150,000."

CHAPTER 11

Friday, March 10, 2023

9:00 AM

From: The Desk of Liz White

My phone rang, it was the governor's office calling.

"Please hold for Governor Miller," his secretary said.

I thought very highly of Simon Miller who always made it his business to chat with me before speaking with Henry.

"Is that Liz White on the line?" The Governor asked.

"It sure is Governor Miller, I hope you're well."

"I am, a little busy with the presidential rumor thing. What do you think, should I run?"

"I'll vote for you so that's one vote."

He laughed.

"I knew I could count on you." He said before changing the subject.

"Liz, this plane crash, the pilot, isn't he a friend of Henry's?"

Uh oh. The governor was the last person I wanted to have this conversation with since there was a chance I was speaking with the next leader of the free world.

"Yes sir, Leighton went to culinary school with him."

"Yes, Leighton the chef, has she ever cooked for you?"

"No sir, not once!"

He laughed again.

"Probably for the best, anyway back to the pilot. Just do me a favor, if the media learns that my family was friendly with umm..."

"Christopher Crimi, sir."

"Yes, Crimi. If they find out, they may come calling so just say you have no comment."

"Yes sir, I will!"

"Thank you, is my son in law there?"

Henry was in his office practicing his golf swing.

CHAPTER 12

Bevy called to tell me Leighton was off the rails. She had Bevy pack a suitcase and Richie drive her to JFK Airport but she had no airline ticket to go anywhere.

"Richie call me to say Mrs. J mad at you for not sending her flight info."

"Flight info to where?"

"I don't know."

"Where is Leighton now?"

"I think she's at the airport."

My cell rang, it was Leighton who likely wanted to tell me something for "my ears only" since she called my cell. All other "non-secretive" calls during business hours were usually made to the landline.

"Leighton? Where are you?"

"I'm off to Palm Beach but I forgot whom I'm flying with. Delta, I hope?"

Leighton's preferred airline was Delta. She despised United and refused to fly on American. She claimed those pilots were lazy and grossly overpaid. I never did come to learn why she felt this way but without much choice, I always avoided booking her a seat on perhaps two of the most convenient airlines to fly.

"Leighton, I haven't booked a flight for you to anywhere, you never asked me to."

"Liz, I really need you checking your email with regularity, last night I sent you instructions."

Scanning my email, I saw nothing. Quickly, I opened Leighton's email and saw a sent email to me but with a message and address that made no sense:

TO: LisWhitee@gmaix.com

Liz,

I need to be in Florida now, so my ticket, book it.

The place.

Leighton

Maybe Leighton hit her head when the plane crashed? Or, more likely she had been functioning at a reduced capacity due to her Ambien habit when she attempted to send me the late-night email.

"Leighton, I have no email from you. Did you check the address?" I asked though I knew the answer.

"I most certainly did." she argued.

Though I could see that her email clearly bounced back, I left it alone, sometimes it was just easier to take the bullet.

I scanned Delta's website for reservations, found a $1300 first class seat on a flight leaving within the hour and booked it.

I gave Leighton the details before asking her if she needed me to book a return ticket.

"Well, DUH!" Leighton said before hanging up.

Not knowing when she planned to return, I tried calling her back but it went straight to voicemail.

CHAPTER 13

Friday, March 10, 2023
10:00 AM
From: The Desk of Liz White

The reports were saying that Christopher Crimi was awake and that doctors were cautiously optimistic that he would make a full recovery. That was good news but that wasn't the story the press was chasing. So, with Leighton on her way to Palm Beach to do God knows what, I prepared for the worst. Soon enough the worst came.

I received a call from a reporter.

"Hi, I'm Mike Rowe, I'm with 1010 WINS NEWS.

Oh shit.

"Yes, what can I do for you?"

"May I speak with Henry Jones."

"What is this regarding, Mr. Rowe?"

"It's confidential but I do believe he should take the call."

Henry was in his office doing pushups, he prided himself on being able to do 50 without a break.

"I'm sorry Mr. Rowe, but Mr. Jones is in a meeting and I cannot interrupt him. Perhaps I can be of some assistance?"

The reporter was quiet for a moment.

"Do you employ a driver, his name is um, Richie Romano?"

Oh crap, Richie, he must have said something to somebody.

"Yes, why are you asking?"

I think Mr. Jones should get in touch with me, ASAP. May I leave my number?"

Richie and his big mouth. Not that he was a bad guy or ever meant to cause an issue, because he never did, but Richie always enjoyed a conversation. Years ago, back when I was still doing a little bit of blow, Richie knew a guy who dealt it so on occasion I'd ask him to pick me up a gram or two. He was usually happy to help out until the time I was actually in the car with him running some errands. I asked Richie if we could make a pickup, but he was hesitant.

"I got to be in Southampton at 9:00 PM sharp to pick up Mrs. J." he reminded me.

"You'll have plenty of time for that. This won't take long, will it?" I asked but it was more of a statement than a question.

He agreed so we took the limo up to Harlem to meet the dealer. Outside the guy's apartment, Richie couldn't find a spot so he parked in front of a hydrant and told me to wait with the car, he'd only be a few minutes. Richie the gabber took more than a few minutes and sure enough a cop started writing a ticket. I jumped out of the car to explain but the cop didn't care. He wrote the ticket and then to my horror a tow truck arrived.

I jumped behind the wheel to move the car but Richie had taken the key! I argued that the driver would be back in a minute but again, no one cared. The car was lifted and with me standing there in stunned disbelief, it was taken away as I desperately texted and called

Richie to get his ass downstairs. Some 10 minutes later, Richie finally returned to find me, but no car.

"What the fuck, Liz?"

"RICHIE DID YOU NOT LOOK AT YOUR PHONE!!!??? THE COPS TOWED THE CAR!" I yelled.

"WHY DIDN'T YOU MOVE THE CAR??!!!" he screamed back.

"BECAUSE YOU TOOK THE KEY!"

He handed me my little bag of cocaine as I called the police to ask where to pick up the damn car. Long story short, it took the two of us three hours and $400.00 but we got it while Leighton of course stewed for hours at the beach club with no driver.

As Richie and I made a beeline to Southampton on the Long Island Expressway, we continued our argument as I took a few toots of the drug.

"How long does it take to buy a gram, Richie? You were up there for 20 minutes!"

"He's a nice guy, he likes to talk turkey." he responded.

"Talk turkey? What the hell does that mean?"

"We do fantasy baseball together, we were talking about our teams."

"Unbelievable Richie, thanks to your silly fantasy baseball, the two of us are probably getting fired!"

"Fantasy baseball? Nope, we're getting fired because of you and your stupid nose candy!"

Richie had a point but I still maintain his gabbing was the real issue at play.

We picked Leighton up but by the time we got there, I must have snorted half the bag. As we returned to Manhattan, I guess I was speaking a mile a minute, something I do when I'm on coke.

"Liz, blah, blah, blah. You sure do talk a lot, right Richie?" Leighton said dismissively.

"She sure does Mrs. J, it's why we were so late!"

With that incident forever ingrained in my brain, I called Richie who was returning to Manhattan after dropping off Leighton at JFK.

"Richie, who did you talk with about the crash?"

"Nobody."

"Nobody? Think Richie, a reporter is asking about you. If Leighton finds out, your ass is grass!"

"I spoke to no one. Not one person."

"Did you speak to anyone at the airport?"

"No one, I just dropped her off at the curb a few minutes ago."

Frustrated, I started to yell.

"RICHIE YESTERDAY, DID YOU TALK TO ANYONE YESTERDAY!"

Henry who was annoyed that he could hear me raise my voice, sat at his desk and frowned, so I whispered...

"Richie, yesterday, before the crash, did anyone at the airport see you?"

"No one, except, well, there was this woman."

"What woman?"

"She wanted to know if Leighton was famous, so yeah, I kind of mentioned that she was the governor's daughter."

Shit double shit!

I hung up the phone and assessed the situation:

1. Leighton was sneaking around with her billionaire friend Christopher when their plane crashed.

2. She managed to escape the scene in a passing taxi.

3. The media was hot on her heels.

4. Henry knew nothing about any of this.

5. I knew, Bevy knew and of course Richie knew.

6. Leighton was on another flight, this time to Florida with access to $150,000, in a real airplane with a real pilot.

7. The governor of New York, and possible presidential candidate, was suggesting, or better yet demanding, that I not tell the media a thing.

8. Christopher was awake according to reports. Would he blow Leighton's cover?

9. Richie told a stranger that Leighton had been to the airport where the crashed flight originated.

As I continued my list, Henry approached me. He had seen the latest report on Christopher.

"Wait until he finds out about his missing passenger!" He said smiling.

Someone had to tell Henry the truth and it certainly wasn't going to be Leighton.

"Henry!" I said louder than I meant to.

"Yes?" He said flexing his biceps, something he liked to do after his push-up regimen.

"It's Leighton, she was the one ..."

I chickened out.

"What about Leighton?"

"Umm, she flew down to Palm Beach this morning."

"Oh. Ok. Does she want me to follow?"

"No, I mean yes, I ..."

"Well, let me know once you decide." he said, sounding frustrated.

Henry, still flexing, walked back to his office, closed the door, sat at his desk and watched CNBC.

CHAPTER 14

Friday, March 10, 2023
1:30 PM
From: The Desk of Liz White

Leighton called from the back of the limo I had waiting for her at the West Palm Beach Airport.

"Liz, where are we going? The driver doesn't know."

"What do you mean, where do you want to go?"

"I guess to the house."

"Whose house?"

"I suppose the Bentley's."

"Are the Bentleys expecting you?"

"I suppose not, you know what, perhaps I'll just come back to New York."

"When?"

"Liz, there's no time like the present."

I booked her another $1,300 first class seat leaving that afternoon. Since she had a few hours to kill I suggested the driver take her to Worth Avenue for shopping and lunch. With access to $150,000, she agreed. I soon began getting alerts on the Citibank account she was using. There was a $22,000 charge at Chanel, another $17,000 at CJLAING and Hermes for a tad over $11,000. One can only assume she dealt with a lazy salesman there.

The reporter, Mike Rowe, called back again asking to speak with Henry.

"Mr. Rowe, I can say with confidence I speak for Mr. Jones. What is it that you wish to know?"

He didn't mince words.

"Was Leighton Jones, the daughter of New York Governor Simon Miller on a plane yesterday that crashed in Rahway, New Jersey?"

"I'm sorry Mr. Rowe, the family does not comment on plane crashes." I said instantly feeling incredibly stupid.

"And your name again? He asked.

"Liz White, I'm Mr. Jones' personal assistant."

Shit.

CHAPTER 15

Friday, March 10, 2023
4:00 PM
From: The Desk of Liz White

I was already thinking about my next job. No way, I would survive this mess. Leighton was acting like a nut as usual but this time the world was potentially tuning in to her shenanigans. She was no longer just my story; she was becoming the biggest news story in town.

My phone rang, it was Leighton.

"Liz, my tennis racquets, were they restrung?"

"Yes, Leighton, they're back at the townhouse and ready to go."

"Oh wonderful! Have Bevy overnight them to me, I'll be needing them."

"Overnight to where? You're coming home tonight, aren't you?"

"There's been a change of plans. Please book me a room at The Breakers. I'll be down here through the weekend."

"Leighton? What do you mean a change of plans?"

Leighton was silent, never a good thing because it meant the explosion was coming.

"Liz! I wasn't asking you a question; I was giving you an order! How after all these years, do we keep having this issue?"

As she ranted, I searched the internet for a reservation at The Breakers, there were none.

"Leighton, there doesn't seem to be a room at the Breakers."

"Who said that?"

"The internet, but I'll make a call. I'll call you right back."

"Liz, do not take no for an answer! Your problem is, you're too nice. Nice doesn't win MY race, Liz!"

"Got it, I'll call you back."

"Don't forget my tennis racquets!" Leighton hung up.

I called the hotel, there were no rooms so I threw her name out there, desperate for something.

"The room is for Leighton Jones, the daughter of New York Governor Simon Miller. Please, anything you can do."

That worked, one room, first floor, nothing great but it was a room. Of course, it was also nonrefundable at $1500. I booked it.

"Leighton, you have a room but it's nothing fancy."

"As long as it's on an upper floor and facing the beach, I'll be fine."

"It's not. It's first floor facing the garden."

Leighton was silent.

"Forget it, I'll just come home. You didn't cancel my flight?"

I hadn't, but the plane was boarding in an hour.

"One hour?!"

Leighton turned her attention to the driver. Speaking very slowly she said,

"Perdo' name senor? I must make a flight rapidamente. Please hurry. Muchas gracias!"

Turning her attention back to me,

"Liz, you and I will discuss this later, have Richie waiting for me at JFK."

"You're flying into LaGuardia, Leighton."

She had already hung up.

CHAPTER 16

Friday, March 10, 2023
5:30 PM
From: The Desk of Liz White

Of course, Leighton missed the flight. As I was trying to find her another one, she stayed on the line, hammering away at me. I was listening to her with one ear.

"Liz, I really need to get out of here. This hotel mess is unacceptable!"

With the other ear, I was listening to Henry who was standing at my desk modeling the various Warby Parker samples that he would never buy.

"Do these work?" he asked strutting around in a pair of thick frames.

"How about these?" swapping the thicker frames for thinner.

"Those are nice, Henry."

"And these?" he asked again, slipping on John Lennon style frames.

"Not for you Henry."

Leighton stopped saying whatever it was she was saying to listen in.

"Liz, what are you talking about?"

"I'm here with Henry, he's trying on some sample frames."

"Glasses?"

"Yes, from Warby Parker."

"What's wrong with his Robert Marc frames?"

"Henry, Leighton prefers you stick with the frames you have."

"Boring!" he shouted, before adding, "Is Leighton still on the line?"

I gave him my "obviously" stare as Leighton continued her rant about my lack of preparation for her last second and completely unnecessary flight to Florida.

"Oh, put her through to my office. I have news for her." Henry said, trying on yet another set of cheap frames.

I completed the reservation; her new flight was set to leave later that evening. I then transferred Leighton to Henry, she was his problem, for now.

CHAPTER 17

Friday, March 10, 2023
6:00 PM
From: The Desk of Liz White

Exhausted, confused and a little freaked out, I just wanted the day to end. With everything going on, I was trying to figure out why Leighton seemingly escaped to Florida only to agree to return because of the "unacceptable" hotel room.

Henry motioned me into his office, he wasn't happy.

"So, umm, I just got off the phone with Leighton. She's rather irate.

Leighton was always irate.

"Is there anything she needs?" I asked knowing that of course there was, there was always something.

"Her seat assignment. She says she looked it up and it's not a window seat."

Leighton only flew first class, but she also insisted on a window seat. So, with everything going on, this was her concern at the moment, the fact that I was unable to procure a window seat.

Henry changed the subject.

"I think I need to call a staff meeting. Does Saturday work for you, Liz?"

Saturday certainly did not work for me but Henry knew this. What was he angling at?

"No," I said, "I have plans this weekend, Henry."

"Plans? A date, I hope. We really do have to find you someone. Richie's son maybe? Richie speaks very highly of him."

Richie's son was in jail for making death threats against his ex-wife. Not to mention, I had a college degree and he dropped out in like the 9th grade. I could go on.

"Thanks Henry, I'll think about it."

Henry studied me up and down as he did from time to time, I'm sure he was still disappointed I wasn't Andrea, his former assistant, the woman I replaced 20 years earlier. In his world, she likely never changed like I did, no gray hair, no expanded waistline, Nope, Andrea probably never aged a day.

She and I worked together for two weeks back when she trained me. Andrea struck me as the stereotypical tough Italian chick from New Jersey, the polar opposite of everyone and better yet anyone Henry had ever met during his privileged life. Andrea had the hair, the perfectly manicured nails, the eye shadow and of course the amazing tits and ass, or at least she did back when she "retired" to raise children. From emails, I saw that Henry and Andrea still conversed a bit. It was usually her talking about her kids and Henry sharing silly jokes or badmouthing me.

Getting back to Henry's request for a staff meeting, I wanted to know why he felt it was necessary when the meeting would just consist of me, Bevy, Richie and two of the housekeepers whom Leighton referred to as the "illegals" despite them having legal documentation to work in the US.

"Henry, why a staff meeting? Is there something you want to say to just me instead?"

"Yes, sit down, this is going to rock your world."

I was already sitting as I pointed out but I knew he finally knew. What a relief! Leighton must have told him her version of the truth. I quickly thought about what my response might be because there was no way he could ever know that I already knew about the crash.

"Liz, on Monday, Simon is announcing his intention to seek the White House! He wants all of us in Albany, the twins too. You may be looking at the next first son, umm, in law. There is such a thing, I think."

Leighton never said a word. The charade would continue.

As I was running all that through my head, Henry kept speaking but I wasn't paying attention. Instead, my focus was on Leighton in Albany. As the world searched for the missing woman, the actual missing woman could be standing right behind her father on a stage as he tells the world he's running for president. Good Grief!

Then there were the twins. How would they get to Albany from their boarding school in New Hampshire? Since they were seniors, they both had their own cars (matching BMWs). However, the girls were deathly afraid of driving on the highway, which was why I had the cars shipped to the school. Perhaps I could find an administrator that would drive them or maybe a friend of theirs who wasn't afraid of roads that could escort them. My mind was racing, searching for a solution.

I explained the girls' transportation issue to Henry who came up with a ridiculous idea.

"There's this black kid I met up there, he's friends with them. He could take them. I'm sure he'd be delighted to drive a new car and meet the future president too! Plus, the optics!" Henry gushed, doing his best to think like a political operative.

The kid Henry was thinking of had a name which I couldn't remember but according to Richie, his father was a Boston Celtics legend. I'm not sure there was anything Henry could have offered that would have "delighted" him.

CHAPTER 18

Friday, March 10th, 2023

6:15 PM

From: The Desk of Liz White

With the big announcement set for Monday, the relaxing weekend I'd hoped for wasn't going to happen so at a little past 6, I rushed out the door with only one thing on my mind, a good stiff drink. In the lobby I was stopped by a man, maybe 10 years older than me; An attractive guy, in a blue-collar sort of way with a bushy mustache that immediately caught my attention.

"Liz White?"

"Yes,"

"I'm Mike Rowe, we spoke earlier."

Shit, it was the reporter.

"Do you have a few minutes to speak? It's rather urgent."

Maybe it was the mustache, maybe the long hair under his San Francisco Giants cap but for whatever reason I said yes and suggested we get a drink. He agreed. There was a Molly Malone's pub just down the block, the place was empty so we took seats at the bar.

Mike offered to buy the first round.

"Are you trying to get me drunk?" I asked.

"No, no absolutely not." he promised.

"Well, in that case, I'll take a beer and a shot of Whiskey."

Mike ordered the same thing for himself. We toasted with the shots, downed them and tapped our beer bottles.

"Liz, I'll be dead honest. The prison, as you know, has video of Leighton Jones leaving the plane. Eventually, it will be enhanced enough with some type of facial recognition to prove it was her. I already know it's her."

What was he expecting me to say?

"So??"

"Can you confirm it was her, Liz?"

"No."

"But you can."

"But I won't."

Mike was inching himself closer to me, I noticed the cologne or maybe the aftershave. I liked the smell; I liked the man. It was the reporter I could do without.

"Liz, please, give me something. You'll remain anonymous. I just need confirmation."

I wasn't about to give Leighton up. I hated her, hated everything about her, who she was, what she stood for but it was my job to protect Leighton and I was very good at it.

"No comment, Mike Rowe." I said polishing off my beer and calling out for another.

"Nothing Liz?"

"I do have something juicy for you, Mr. Reporter."

"What is it," he said leaning in even closer, our noses, almost touching.

"You'll have to get me drunk first."

Mike smiled; I couldn't resist so I kissed him.

We decided to go back to his place and sure enough he had the one thing I swore I'd never do again, cocaine.

It's not that I was an addict, far from it, but coke and me, it was kind of like oil and water. I did it, I loved it, but "coke nights" were never a great thing. For starters I can't shut the fuck up when I'm on it. So as the two of us shared a few lines, I of course forgot to keep my big mouth closed.

CHAPTER 19

Saturday, March 11th, 2023

7:30 AM

From: The Desk of Liz White

I awoke in a fog. What time was it? 7:30 AM. Where was I? Oh shit, the reporter, Mike Rowe, I was at his place, under the covers and yeah, not wearing a thing. I tried to remember what we discussed. I was bitching about Andrea, Henry's ex-secretary, being better looking than me. For some reason, I was really steamed about that and thanks to the coke, I decided to vent.

We also discussed the charity work Leighton and Henry were involved with which bored the shit out of Mike. I searched for my phone; I had the presence of mind to turn it off just in case my fuck buddy reporter decided to take a peek. I powered back up, five emails from Leighton, each one just a little less coherent than the prior one. To summarize, she could not imagine why I wasn't getting back to her and perhaps the best one liner of them all,

"I am emailing a person who IS HOPEFULLY DEAD!"

According to the emails, after getting to the airport Leighton apparently decided to have the driver take her back to The Breakers, lousy room and all. That's where she must have spent the night.

I quietly started emailing her back so as not to wake Mike.

"Leighton, so sorry, went to bed under the weather. I'm feeling better now."

Truthfully, I went to bed feeling great but now I felt under the weather or more accurately, I felt like shit. My phone rang, of course the ringer was on, waking Mike up. It was Leighton.

"Liz? I've been emailing you! Dozens! You have no right to ignore me, sick or not!"

"Leighton, hold on," I began saying which naturally piqued Mike's interest.

"No, Liz, you hold on! I was nearly killed in a plane crash a few days ago, I'm lucky to be alive."

Whoa! A major admission from Leighton as the reporter tracking the story was rubbing his penis against my asshole. I jumped out of bed and made my way to the living room. I started pacing completely nude until Mike slipped a bathrobe on me.

"Leighton, what are you telling me?"

"No one can know this, not Henry, not my father, no one."

Mike looked at me.

"What's she saying?" he asked loud enough that Leighton could hear him.

"Are you with someone, Liz?" Leighton asked.

"I am Leighton, I'm with a friend."

"Ooh, a friend, sexy time?"

"Leighton, he's just a friend."

"Well, it's about time you had a friend. Henry and I are always talking about it! You've been with us, what now? 11-12 years and never once have you mentioned a boyfriend or girlfriend, we're progressive, we don't judge."

"Leighton, I've been with you 20 years and I like men."

Mike was all smiles, still listening in and taking notes on a small pad. The only thing missing was one of those hats with a sign that said, "Press." I tried waving him off but he ignored me.

"Anyway, Liz," Leighton said changing the subject, "Here's a small world thing for you. So, my driver yesterday, when he's not driving in a car, he's a pro tennis player from Brazil or Peru, somewhere like that. We wound up having a few drinks back at the hotel and it looks like he and I are going to be playing tennis this afternoon, so I will need my racquets after all."

This was hardly the first time Leighton decided to have a platonic relationship and I say platonic because I can't imagine it being anything but with a hired hand. She's done this before with florists, manicurists and even a gardener. What did surprise me was her thinking I could magically get her tennis gear to Florida from New York within a few hours.

"Leighton, I can't get you the racquets that quickly."

"But you can!" she insisted. "Fly them down yourself! If you leave now, you can be here by 1PM, but you better get moving."

Leighton was potentially right; I could do that but I didn't want to.

"Leighton, I can't just drop everything and fly down to meet you today."

"And why not?"

"Just because."

"Liz, bring your racquet too, we'll find a fourth and make it doubles!"

"Leighton! I have a life too."

"Liz, we both know you're lying. See ya soon, gotta pop!"

Mike wanted to know what Leighton said to me. To distract him, I pulled his dick out of his boxers and gave him a blowjob. The things I'll do to protect Leighton. As I was leaving the reporter's place after an unusual but rather exciting overnight, he begged again.

"Liz, give me something! A tip, I need this, Liz!"

I kissed him on the mouth before leaving his place.

"Liz! Please!"

"I'm not sure what you want, Mike. I slept with you, heck, I just gave you a blowjob but still you want more?"

"Liz, anything, I'm anchoring on the radio in two hours, it's a big deal to me, I don't get a chance to anchor often."

"Mike, on Monday, 1:00 PM sharp from Albany, the governor is announcing his candidacy for president. Leighton and Henry will be there but you didn't hear that from me."

Aired March 11, 2023 - 10:00 AM ET

THIS IS A RUSH RADIO TRANSCRIPT: THIS COPY MAY NOT BE IN ITS FINAL FORM AND MAY BE UPDATED.

[10:00:00]

MIKE ROWE: 1010 WINS NEWS ANCHOR: *A 1010 WINS NEWS exclusive! I'm Mike Rowe, filling in for Bob LeMoullec on the anchor desk and here's what's happening. New York Governor Simon Miller plans to announce his candidacy for President of the United States on Monday afternoon according to a source close to the second term governor. He'll be surrounded by family as he seeks to become the first New York governor to become president since Franklin Delano Roosevelt. He's currently polling well nationally but some New Yorkers we spoke to earlier today have mixed feelings.*

(SOUNDBITES)

MAN ON STREET: I'd vote for him but he's a tax and spend liberal. That's not good.

WOMAN ON STREET: He's a bored rich man, a rich man wasting everyone's time.

WOMAN ON STREET #2: I love him! Maybe I'll marry him and become first lady!

MIKE ROWE: 1010 WINS NEWS ANCHOR: *Miller, who is 73 lost his wife Sally to breast cancer eight years ago, just one year after he decided to leave his successful law practice and run for governor. In other news, The Italian Plate CEO Christopher Crimi has regained consciousness and appears on his way to making a full recovery following last week's small plane crash. Investigators are hoping he might shed some light on his missing passenger, the woman seen leaving the crash site after she pulled him from the wreckage. Her disappearance has the nation talking.*

CHAPTER 20

Saturday, March 11, 2023

10:00 AM

From: The Desk of Liz White

Without a shower, and likely smelling of sex and booze, I made the 10AM flight out of JFK with Leighton's tennis racquets in hand. I did buy myself a first-class ticket for $1,400. Screw it, Henry was paying after all.

It was only my second time flying first class so I'd be lying if I said I wasn't at least a little excited. Being called on to pre-board was only part of the thrill. The other part was seeing the passengers forced to fly in coach being ushered past me as I sat in luxury. Unfortunately, the fun and games came to an abrupt end when I looked up and saw Henry frowning.

"Liz?"

"Henry, I uh." I stuttered.

"First class? Perhaps we should renegotiate your pay." he said as he filed past me and past the curtain into coach.

Henry loved "being cheap". He might pay 33 million dollars for a townhouse in Manhattan, another 14 million for a place in Southampton, another 4.5 million for a hunting cabin upstate but when it came to flying, there he drew the line. If he could save money flying coach, he would do it. Leighton had no such qualms flying first class and thought Henry foolish for sitting in "tourist class" as she called it.

He had also recently taken to booking his own flights. When I asked him why, he pulled out his phone and showed me his airline app, explaining it to me as if I had never seen one. Henry did this sort of thing. In his world, if it was new to him that meant it was new to me too.

As I sat in first class with my boss tucked in the rear somewhere it dawned on me, the only reason I was even on the plane was to deliver the tennis racquets. With everyone seated but the doors still open, I made a split-second decision and charged the rear of the airplane.

"Henry! Come with me!" I hollered loud enough to startle the other passengers.

"Liz?"

"Henry, there's a seat for you in first. Let's go!"

"I'm fine here Liz, I have an aisle seat."

"Henry! Please!" I shouted knowing that as soon as they closed the doors, I was going to Florida despite no longer needing to.

Henry refused to budge, so I hustled back to my seat, grabbed the bag of racquets from the overhead bin and sprinted again to Henry.

"These are Leighton's! Please deliver them to her, I have to run! I'm getting off the plane!" I shouted at Henry, much to his distaste.

I made a run for the exit as the flight attendant desperately tried to get me to take my seat. Just as another attendant was about to seal the door shut, I pushed past her onto the jetway.

With Florida no longer on my afternoon schedule, I leisurely walked through JFK. I passed a bar that was airing a news program. Christopher Crimi was being interviewed. It was some type of press conference. Wearing sunglasses and a bandage on his forehead he was asked about Leighton.

Reporter: "The woman seen leaving the plane, who was she?"

Christopher: "As I told investigators, I don't recall the crash or anything leading up to it."

Reporter: "So, you can't remember who you were flying with?"

Christopher: "I don't recall the crash or anything leading up to it."

Reporter: "Text messages? Emails? You must have shared some type of correspondence with the person who got on your plane and flew with you?"

Christopher: "This has been traumatic, I'm lucky to be alive, I'm happy no one else was hurt."

A woman, I guess, Christopher's lawyer told the room that would be the last question. Christopher was helped up from the table where he was seated and walked off as reporters shouted more questions. The two things I learned: He was fine and most importantly, he was covering for Leighton.

CHAPTER 21

I tried getting an Uber but my account had been suspended, Leighton's fault. A few days before the crash, she was mad at Richie for some reason and refused to ride with him so she called me from the townhouse demanding I have a car service waiting for her. I sent an Uber Black her way. Leighton apparently had words with the driver who wasn't happy that she kept him waiting. Some type of argument ensued and she was kicked out of the car and of course since I ordered the ride, my account was blocked.

So instead, I waited in an incredibly long line for a yellow taxi to take me back to Manhattan. I had taken the subway to the airport but I was tired, I only wanted to close my eyes for a few minutes, a car just seemed like a great idea. I killed time by reading the news on my phone; the top story, Christopher Crimi was awake but not talking about his passenger, that I already knew. The other top story, rumors from an unnamed source (me) that Governor Miller would be announcing his run for the presidency on Monday.

Meanwhile, as it hit me that I was in the middle of two major news stories, a woman tried cutting in, pretending she didn't understand the rules of waiting on line.

"THERE'S A LINE HERE!" I yelled.

The woman didn't take kindly to me calling her out so she shoved me out of her way. I pushed back, a cop came out of nowhere and separated us.

"OK, ladies, more of that and you're going to get arrested!"

Looking at me, he repeated the threat.

"You want to get arrested, Miss?"

"Me? She cut the line! Why are you threatening me?"

"Because you hit first!"

"I did not!" I argued as my phone rang; it was Leighton.

"Excuse me officer, but this is Governor Simon Miller's daughter calling. Do you mind if I answer it?" I said in my most affected voice.

"Hello Leighton."

The officer seemed to be enjoying the moment. Perhaps it was seeing two women shove each other or, perhaps he believed me when I told him who was calling but for whatever reason, he refused to drop it.

"We're not done here." he said as I attempted to wave him away.

"Liz, what's that commotion? Where are you? On the plane with my tennis racquets, I hope."

"Liz, Henry has them, I saw him on the plane."

"The plane? So, you're on the plane too?"

"No, Leighton, once I saw ..."

The officer was staring at me rather intently.

"Leighton, can you hold on a moment?"

I took the phone away from my ear to address the annoying cop.

"Is there something more you need officer?"

"I want to make sure you understand ..." he started to say but I could hear Leighton's voice so I put the phone back up to my ear.

"Leighton."

"Liz, whom are you speaking with?"

"Leighton, it's this cop. I'm waiting for a taxi and some woman cut the line, she and I had words, this cop won't leave me alone. I even told him who you are."

"I'll speak with him, hand him your phone, Liz."

"Leighton Jones would like a word with you."

"Who?

"Governor Miller's daughter."

The cop took the phone.

"Hello? Yes, I mean, yes, OK, my apologies Madam, please give the governor my best."

He handed me back my phone and walked off.

"Leighton? Thank you," I began to say.

"Liz, what have I told you over and over? Don't be so nice. Nice never wins."

"I wasn't being nice; I was being a bitch." I said defensively.

"Liz, sometimes you need to kill them with kindness too."

I updated Leighton on the latest including the press conference with Christopher but she quickly cut me off saying she wasn't
interested. Instead, we discussed Monday and specifically the twins
who I explained didn't feel comfortable driving on their own because
they were afraid of highways. Therefore, the decision was made by
me that Richie would drive up from New York to pick them up from
New Hampshire and drive them to Albany.

Leighton wasn't keen on the idea.

"So, if Richie is with the girls, who's driving me to Albany?"

"I thought I could get you a flight directly into Albany from
Palm Beach, Leighton."

"No, that doesn't work, I need to get back to the city for a color,
extension and cut. Has my hair arrived from London?"

Leighton was particular about her hair extensions. Every two
months or so new hair was flown in but I wasn't sure when the last
batch arrived.

Climbing into the back of the taxi, I searched my emails for a
delivery confirmation. Yes! A delivery was made a week or so earlier
but I wasn't convinced I could get Frederic to drop everything in
order to doll up Leighton for Albany.

"The hair is here, Leighton, but Frederic, he might be
a problem."

"Just get me back to New York on Sunday, have him meet me
Monday morning at let's say 4AM."

Sure, make a last second call to one of the busiest and most
well-known hairdressers in New York City to book a house call at
4AM. No problem.

Frederic's client list included the likes of Barbara Streisand, Meryl Streep and even Mick Jagger. He didn't need Leighton but she could be charming when she had to and she charmed Frederic. Still, this was more than just a last second request and on top of that, it would be at an ungodly hour.

I called Frederic and explained the situation. Leighton was originally in Florida for a reason I still didn't understand but now she was still there to play tennis with a limo driver; just a few days before her father was about to make the biggest political announcement of his life.

Frederic listened patiently.

"So, what time does she need me?"

"4AM, Monday morning."

"Her bedroom again, Liz? Oh dear."

"Would you prefer another room, Frederic?"

"Obviously Liz, I mean, her bedroom, there are bodies buried in there, I'm sure."

Frederic wasn't exaggerating. Despite having housekeepers employed seven days a week, Leighton's bedroom was always a train wreck. Between clothing, shoes, jewelry and prescription meds it was a house of horrors. Bevy, normally a strong woman, would call me crying as she tried to make heads or tails of the room only to have Leighton storm in, have a temper tantrum and dump out all her dresser drawers.

CHAPTER 22

I decided to make a pit stop at the townhouse to help Bevy organize. A little about the place. A six-story building on the corner of Park and 78th Street, some of the neighbors included Al Pacino and Lady Gaga. The 6th floor, which you could reach via elevator, was for the twins. Leighton used the 4th and 5th floors and Henry the 3rd floor. The second floor included a kitchen, living room, family room and dining room. The first floor was for the help, it had a kitchen too and some bedrooms. Leighton called it the cellar.

I knew Leighton would be disappointed if Frederic refused to do her hair in the bedroom so I attempted to straighten it up with Bevy's help. As to be expected, it looked like a bomb had gone off. Bevy said she spent a few hours working on the place but still had a long way to go so she was grateful for my assistance. As I dug through shopping bags of new clothing along with packages of more new clothing, I came across a huge diamond ring lying on the floor.

"Bevy, look what I found."

Bevy nearly broke into tears.

"Oh good! Mrs. J, she say I stole ring. I did not steal it, she lost it. She always doing that. My sister say I should quit but I don't think Mrs. J will let me."

Leighton had the rare ability to blame everyone for her failures, to the point where one would have to be crazy to stay with her. But she also had the ability to scare the shit out of you for even thinking about leaving. Then there was charming Leighton. The woman who could befriend a limo driver or charm a hairdresser or in my case, a policeman.

As we cleaned her room, my phone rang, it was Mike Rowe, the reporter.

"Yes, Mike."

"I have the proof. A second witness. Leighton was on the plane. I know you know but I wanted you to know that I know too."

Shit.

"When do you plan to report this?"

"In 15 minutes."

Aired March 11, 2023 - 12:45 AM ET

THIS IS A RUSH RADIO TRANSCRIPT. THIS COPY MAY NOT BE IN ITS FINAL FORM AND MAY BE UPDATED.

[12:45:00]

MIKE ROWE: 1010 WINS NEWS ANCHOR: You're listening to 1010 WINS NEWS! I'm Mike Rowe filling in this afternoon for Bob LeMoullec on the anchor desk. Our top story. Last week's small plane crash involving The Italian Plate founder, Christopher Crimi, well, we now know the name of the missing passenger and she is Leighton Jones, the daughter of New York Governor, Simon Miller. Not only has Ms. Jones been identified but so has her handbag. According to experts, it's a Hermes Birkin 35, valued at $112,000. Ms. Jones, who is married to Wall Street financier, Henry Jones, was apparently uninjured during last Monday's crash. She was seen pulling Crimi safely from the wreckage before leaving the scene via taxi. We have reached out to reps. for Ms. Jones and the Governor's office for comment but so far, no word from either party.

CHAPTER 23

Saturday, March 11, 2023
1:00 PM
From: The Desk of Liz White

Frantically, I called Leighton to give her a heads up that she was the top news story, but she cut me off before I could speak.

"Liz! I have to tell you that Ernesto, I believe that's his name. Excuse me, it's Ernesto, correct?"

I heard a man with an accent correct her. "Call me Ernie."

"Yes, Ernie, like Ernie and Bert, noted." Leighton said before turning her attention back to me. "Liz, Ernesto is a wonderful player. I would like to fly him up for the doubles tournament next month at Piping Rock, please see to it."

This wasn't unusual. At some of the competitive tennis matches at the various clubs and organizations Leighton and Henry belonged to, finding "ringers" as I called them, wasn't frowned upon. Leighton used ringers for years including the very handsome and very athletic David from Las Vegas.

We would fly David in for a mixed doubles tournament that Leighton was playing in, be it in the city or the Hamptons. His going rate was $10,000 per tournament, win or lose. I really liked David from Las Vegas but he got married and retired from whoring out his tennis skills.

Leighton was trying to wrap up our phone call but I still needed to deliver the news.

"Leighton??!!" I yelled. "Don't hang up!"

"Liz, have I not told you when I'm playing tennis, I am never available. I just happened to be taking a sip of water when I saw my phone exploding."

"Wait, Henry brought you your tennis racquets?" I asked, surprised that she would ever attempt to play without them.

"No, he did not, I had to borrow one and it's aggravating my tennis elbow but Ernesto needed to play earlier than I had hoped. Got to go!"

Leighton hung up. I called back, frantic. Luckily, she picked up again.

"Liz?"

"Leighton, don't hang up! There's a news report claiming it was you on the plane."

"Am I the lead story?"

"I'm sure you will be."

Leighton was making this clicking sound with her tongue that she made when she was thinking.

"Liz, it's best that I keep a low profile. Can you arrange a private jet to take me home? I'd hate to be hounded at the airport. I've never been one to seek attention. I'll be off the courts within the hour…"

Henry called, interrupting the conversation with Leighton, he had arrived at the West Palm Beach Airport but was unsure how I planned to have him rendezvous with his wife.

"Henry, you never mentioned needing my help, I didn't even know you were flying to Florida until I saw you on the plane."

I was met with silence.

"Henry, you do have Leighton's tennis racquets?"

"Umm, uh."

"Henry, you forgot her racquets, didn't you?"

"Yes, I never gave it a second thought after the flight attendant stowed them."

Shit, we had just spent thousands of dollars getting those racquets restrung and the new grips just like Leighton liked them. I would have to deal with the airline's lost and found, never an easy experience. But, for now, I had a much bigger issue.

"Henry, have you seen the news?"

"Of course, I've seen the news, I've been up for hours."

It was clear he hadn't heard "the news" so I was trying to figure out the best way to let Henry know his wife was on her way to becoming the biggest news story of I guess the week, maybe even the month when my phone buzzed, it was Leighton again on the other line.

"Henry, Leighton is calling me, can you hold?"

"Liz, I need you to call me a car…"

"Please hold Henry!" "Yes, Leighton!"

"Liz, Henry should be arriving soon. Have him wait at the airport; Ernesto is driving me back now. Did you arrange a plane?"

I had not, I was busy dealing with Henry.

"Leighton, Henry landed, he's waiting for a car. Perhaps you can reach out to him directly?" I begged.

"I don't think that's a very good idea, right now. I'm frustrated, he'll be frustrated. You fill him in on my situation. In the meantime, get me a plane."

"Leighton, it will have to be commercial. I can't just snap my fingers and get you a private jet. That takes time."

Leighton hung up aggravated. I got back to Henry.

"Henry? You still there?"

"I am Liz, and I have to say I'm quite annoyed!"

Leighton was mad at me, Henry was mad at me, and, for the record, it was supposed to be my day off.

"Henry, something has happened and you need to know."

"Is it serious? The twins?"

"No, it's not the twins."

Well actually I had an issue with the twins too. Richie sent me a text. He was in contact with the girls, letting them know he would be arriving Sunday afternoon to get them to Albany on Sunday night where they would stay at a hotel I arranged. However, despite having perhaps over $100,000 worth of designer clothing that I had shipped to their school, neither felt they had anything appropriate to wear for their grandfather's presidential announcement. They were demanding Richie pick them up and drive them back to the townhouse where they could find something suitable to wear. Richie agreed, so now his plan was to get them back to the city Sunday night instead. From there, I would have to figure out how to get the family of four to Albany for Monday's noon announcement. I wasn't sure having

Richie drive all of them up Monday morning would be satisfactory for any of them.

Despite all this, I decided to keep Henry out of that loop, instead I briefed him on Leighton's situation.

"Henry, the media knows who Christopher's passenger was."

"Well, that's not a story I have much interest in, Liz."

"Henry, the missing passenger is Leighton."

CHAPTER 24

Saturday, March 11, 2023
1:30 PM
From: The Desk of Liz White

"I had a feeling it might be her." Henry said as he attempted to reassure himself that he was still master of his universe.

I knew he was shaken. Henry wasn't dumb, far from it, but he rarely knew what was going on around him; or more accurately, he had little interest in knowing what was going on around him. Keeping track of all that was my job.

"Do you think Leighton was having a fling with the guy?"

Sure, she might have been and her emails seem to suggest it. Although in my 20 years with Leighton, she had pulled some rather substantial bullshit, as far as I could tell she had remained loyal to Henry and there was even a great deal of love between the two of them.

"I don't know Henry. I'm sure it was platonic, two old friends."

"Then, why didn't she tell me?" he asked sounding like a lost child looking for his mother.

"Henry, maybe ..."

He cut me off.

"I know, she didn't want me to worry about her flying in a small plane, which I would have. I don't like them. Did I tell you about the time I went skydiving?"

He had, many times. Years earlier, in the Bahamas. He met up with an old friend from his Harvard days. They smoked some marijuana, which Henry rarely did, and then decided to go skydiving. Henry figured between training and what not, he'd be back to normal mentally before the jump but this was the Bahamas we're talking about. They fitted him with a suit, introduced him to his tandem partner and some 45 minutes after getting good and stoned, he was falling from a height of 16,000 feet. Henry said it was the dumbest and most terrifying ordeal of his life.

I reminded Henry that his skydiving adventure was a scary time but there was nothing wrong with the plane. After giving it some thought, he agreed that his skydiving story wasn't relevant.

I sent Henry back into the airport and advised him to wait at the Delta Club where I would have Leighton meet him. Meanwhile, I booked them two first class seats to Philadelphia since the New York flights were sold out. I then arranged a car to drive them back into Manhattan.

I called Leighton with the flight details. Of course, she was not happy.

"Philadelphia??? No to Philadelphia! I want to go to New York! Have you seen the news? I need to get home!"

I explained the situation. It was Saturday, there were only a certain number of flights each day to the various cities around the world. It was the reason the airlines recommended advanced reservations but to Leighton the airline business may as well have been her subway, always running, 24/7.

CHAPTER 25

Saturday, March 11, 2023

4:00 PM

From: The Desk of Liz White

I arrived home exhausted but before I could even take my shoes off Bevy called; she had a problem. Richie told her that he had the twins but Jackie, the more annoying of the two, had decided she was now gluten free and needed her special diet requirements met. Of all the things the Jones family insisted upon, gluten free was never on the list so Bevy was unsure of what to do.

"Liz, maybe you go to market for me. You eat that stuff, I never do."

The last thing I wanted to do was go food shopping and then deliver it to the townhouse but Bevy was desperate so off I went. I googled gluten free breakfasts, lunches and dinners and assuming google was right, filled a cart with everything I could find that was labeled gluten free. With four shopping bags, I hailed a taxi to the townhouse to deliver the food.

"Bevy, hopefully you can make something out of all this." I said, dumping the products on the kitchen counter.

"I don't know, Liz, gluten free is stupid but I try."

CHAPTER 26

Sunday, March 12, 2023
7:00 AM
From: The Desk of Liz White

Sunday, peaceful Sunday. I assumed Leighton and Henry were home from Florida, via Philadelphia. The Twins were on their way back too from New Hampshire and I had some me time before the clock struck 6AM, Monday morning, and I'd be transported back into the world of Leighton.

Wrong again Liz. Opening my phone, I was already back.

The top story I'd dreaded was now breaking news — everywhere.

"Park Ave. Socialite is The Missing Woman."

"She Saved the Pilot and Then She Saved the Handbag."

"Hero Billionaire Bimbo?"

There were also the less sensationalistic headlines.

"Daughter of NY Governor is the Missing Woman"

"Who is Leighton Jones?"

As I read the dozens of articles related to the crash, I learned that Christopher was released from the hospital and quickly left the country back to his native Italy, still refusing to say much of anything.

Meanwhile, the memes, yep, Leighton was a meme. I saw the very first one on Twitter. Thankfully, Leighton didn't do Twitter, Facebook or even Instagram which was a good thing considering her twins' behavior on social media. Skirts too short, parties a little too late, boys, plenty of boys.

The meme was Leighton running from the crash with the red soled heels and Hermes Birkin in hand. It said, "Late for my connecting flight!" It wasn't funny but I was sure it wouldn't be the last meme either.

I turned my attention to the news programs, expecting to see more of Leighton when my cell rang, it was Henry.

"Liz, I am umm, remember we spoke about the NDA thing?"

I did but still, I had no idea why he broached the subject in the first place especially considering it was before he knew of the crash.

"Yes, Henry, what about it?"

"Well, I guess with all that's going on now with Leighton and the crash and her father, we think you should sign one."

"We" usually meant "Henry." If he wanted me to do something that he knew might annoy me, he'd add "we" as in Leighton and Henry but it was never Leighton and Henry. I knew from the emails, from Bevy and Richie, from every form of whatever communication link they shared, not once would the two of them ever discuss a matter face to face. No, "in person" time was for eating, traveling or entertaining. Nothing of significance other than the girls was ever discussed, meaning Leighton and Henry most certainly did not discuss me signing an NDA.

I pressed Henry for clarification.

"Henry, you originally asked me about signing an NDA before we knew Leighton was involved in the crash (or before he did at least). Why did we discuss it then?" I asked.

Henry took a deep breath.

"Liz, what I tell you now does not leave the room."

Since we were each at our own home, there was actually more than just one room involved but I left that alone.

"Yes, Henry, what is it?"

"I may have, well I, shit, remember Andrea?"

His beloved ex-secretary.

"Yes, Andrea, of course. What about her?"

"I umm, I…, and again this is why I really should have made sure we were NDA'd but anyway, I am, I am, having a thing with Andrea and umm, her husband, he, I think, he found out."

"A thing? What does that mean?"

"Liz, listen closely to what I am saying because I don't care to repeat myself."

"Yes, Henry, I'm listening."

"I've been well, I've been having phone sex with Andrea for quite some time."

What? Henry had never once in 20 years shocked or surprised me; Leighton did daily but never like this and certainly not as graphically.

Oddly enough I found myself a little jealous. Not that I wanted phone sex with my boss, but more to the point that he was having whatever that was with the woman I replaced. A woman, by the way, who wasn't nearly as competent or as dedicated as me but I needed to move past Henry's X-rated adventures, so I tried somewhat to change the focus of his concerns.

"Henry, if this were to break now, I'm the least of your worries, you do understand that, right? Leighton, Governor Miller, obviously Andrea's husband, her family, your kids! Heck, Richie the big mouth! Why are we having this conversation?"

Henry didn't disagree. I promised him that his secret was safe with me.

"How are you getting to Albany?" he asked, just as I was about to hang up.

"Me, why would I be going?"

"Oh, I was certain it was mentioned, Simon requested you personally. He thinks very highly of you."

I was flattered.

"Thank you, Henry, that means a lot." I gushed.

"Don't thank me, I didn't invite you, Simon did."

Henry hung up.

CHAPTER 27

Sunday, March 12, 2023
3:00 PM
From: The Desk of Liz White

I spoke to Richie; he was returning to New York with the girls safely tucked in the back of the limo. Leighton and Henry were safely stowed away at the townhouse as well. All I needed to do was make sure the four of them got into Richie's car Monday morning for the ride to Albany. I was feeling good about all of it until Richie threw me a curveball.

"So, the girls are asking who's doing their hair for Monday. What ya got lined up for that?"

Shit, the girls' hair!! Damn it!

Frederic was set to arrive at 4AM Monday morning to do Leighton's extensions and a cut in her bedroom. Could he come earlier to bang out the twins' too? I would have to find out but I'd also have to make sure the girls could handle a let's say 2AM wake up call. I wasn't sure that was something either of them could pull off.

Then I had to think about getting myself to Albany too. I didn't own a car and I most certainly had no intention of driving up with the family. No way! As I was sorting all that out, Mike Rowe called.

"Liz, I'll be in Albany tomorrow. I wanted you to know, I do plan to pepper Leighton with questions."

"Seriously, Mike, the nation is in dire straits and needs leadership, but Leighton, she's your focus?"

"Yes," was all he said.

"Mike, how are you getting to Albany?"

"I'm driving up in the morning."

"Can you give me a lift?"

"It's a date!"

Mike agreed to pick me up from my apartment so that was one problem solved. Of course, a few hours in a car with a reporter looking to destroy my boss was a conflict of interest but I really needed the lift.

I then reached out to Frederic and explained the situation with the twins.

"I'll work with Jackie but not Michelle." He said.

"What, why?"

"She bit me, remember?"

Shit.

It was true, Michelle did bite Frederic but she was like five at the time.

"Frederic, what would it take for you to do Michelle's hair too? Name your price."

"$2,000"

"Done!"

So, Leighton's haircut plus extensions would run $3000, Jackie's $1,000 and Michelle (the biter) would be $2,000. Six grand in hairdos, only in New York.

CHAPTER 28

Monday, March 13, 2023

4:00 AM

From: The Desk of Liz White

Mike Rowe woke me up at the ungodly hour of 4AM. He and I were planning to meet up at 7:30 AM for the ride to Albany.

"Liz, remember when we went back to my place?"

"Mike, obviously."

"Liz, you might hate me for this but remember what you told me about Henry's old assistant, Andrea?"

I knew what he was about to say wasn't going to be good but I tried playing it cool.

"Not really, Mike."

"Well, you said that you knew Henry and Andrea had carried on a friendship."

Oh shit, loose lips, sink ships! As I mentioned before, I wasn't a fan of the relationship Henry had with Andrea over the years but until my last phone call with Henry, I never knew the extent of it. Had I, in a drunken and coked up state, said something really stupid?

"Mike, Henry is a good man, he's decent to people including people who used to work for him. I hope when I was quite drunk, and fucking you by the way, I didn't say something rude about either of them." I said sternly into the phone.

"Liz, we have Andrea's husband on tape telling us that his soon to be ex-wife had a, how do I say this, a sordid affair with Henry including rough sex."

"What??!! What the hell are you talking about?"

"Can you confirm or deny allegations that Henry and Andrea were involved in some type of sexual relationship that included S&M themed activities."

"Fuck you, Mike."

I hung up.

Shit, shit, shit, shit, shit!!

Aired March 13, 2023 - 6:00 AM ET

THIS IS A RUSH RADIO TRANSCRIPT. THIS COPY MAY NOT BE IN ITS FINAL FORM AND MAY BE UPDATED.

[6:00]

BOB LEMOULLEC: 1010 WINS NEWS ANCHOR: It's 6AM, Monday morning and you're listening to 1010 WINS NEWS! all news, all the time! I'm Bob LeMoullec, and here's what's happening! Leighton Jones, you probably know the name by now. Last we heard she survived a small plane crash being piloted by her friend, The Italian Plate founder, Christopher Crimi. Well, now it looks like her husband has a friend too. 1010 WINS NEWS reporter Mike Rowe has that story."

MIKE ROWE: 1010 WINS NEWS REPORTER: Good morning, Bob, yeah, so uh, I'm headed up to Albany where New York Governor Simon Miller is expected to announce his candidacy for President of the United States. Meanwhile, his family is dealing with some controversy surrounding his daughter, Leighton Jones, who allegedly survived a plane crash just last week. Eyewitness reports indicate a woman, now believed to be Mrs. Jones, left the scene of the crash before rescue crews arrived. Now, on top of that, we have reports that her husband, Wall Street investment banker, Henry Jones, could be in hot water too. Gio Amadola claims that his wife, Andrea Amadola, from whom he's currently separated, had a sordid affair with Jones that included, well, plenty of bondage themed activities. *Andrea Amadola was once an assistant to Jones but according to Gio, she did more than just assist him. Here's some of what Mr. Amadola said earlier during an exclusive interview.*

(SOUNDBITE)

GIO AMADOLA: She had whip marks, she had scratches, when I'd ask her who'd done it to her, she'd cry and say it was Henry. He was never nice to her, a real bad guy, very bad!

MIKE ROWE: 1010 WINS NEWS REPORTER: We have reached out to a rep for Leighton and Henry Jones for comment but at this hour, nothing yet. I'm Mike Rowe, 1010 WINS NEWS!

CHAPTER 29

Monday, March 13, 2023
6:30 AM
From: The Desk of Liz White

Yep, Monday morning. Leighton and the crash were no longer the talk of the town. The scandal involving Henry Jones and Andrea and her sudden separation from her husband Gio of 25 years was now breaking news thanks to claims he made about his wife's alleged ugly affair.

Bevy called me once she learned of the news.

"Liz, no good, no good this morning. Mr. J, no good. He mad, say news is lying. Mrs. J, she getting hair done, she don't know yet. She won't like it either."

This was my fault. I told Mike about Andrea when I was drunk and high. I most certainly did not say they were sleeping together or beating each other but I clearly gave the dickhead reporter the lead.

My call with Bevy was interrupted by the governor's office.

"Please hold for Governor Miller."

"Liz?"

"Yes Governor, good morning."

"You're the smartest person at your office so that's why I'm coming to you first."

I appreciated the compliment but my office was just Henry and me so I'm not sure it was meant to be flattery.

"Liz, is this affair stuff for real? I gotta know, between this and Leighton, I'm falling behind in the headlines. Please, Liz, tell me what you know."

"Governor, I swear, I do not know of any sexual-stuff (I wished I used a better term) between Henry and anyone, let alone Andrea."

"I see, when did she work for Henry?"

"Years ago, I replaced her back in 2001."

"Hmm, Liz, has Henry ever attempted to force himself on you?"

"No sir, not once, not ever!" I stated with certainty.

"Ok, I guess I could see that."

"Gee thanks, Governor."

That got a chuckle out of Governor Miller but this was a serious situation. I told him I would be in Albany later today for the big announcement. He thanked me for my support before signing off.

I wasn't lying to the governor. Henry never once in our 20 years working together ever gave me a second look. However, there was a period of time when he rudely called me "Hamper Girl"; unhappy with my often-wrinkled clothing which actually led to me being set up to appear on a reality television show called *What Not to Wear*.

It was a few years earlier, I had been returning from lunch, right in front of our office building when I was stopped by a younger gay man and I guess you could say voluptuous woman, both holding microphones as a camera person rolled. A big deal was made of me as I was peppered with questions about my wardrobe. Flattered, I discussed my attire, bragging about my everyday "uniform," denim pants, a sleeveless purple top and a cardigan. The crew thanked me for my time before quickly packing up and leaving.

I was proud of myself, believing I was stopped because of my fashion sense but also a little confused by the encounter until a few days later when I received a call from a show producer. I was told my stylings were "unique and eccentric" but they also felt they could do more for me so they offered a makeover and $7,000 in free clothing if I agreed to be on their program. As I spoke over the phone, still trying to figure out how they got my number, Henry approached my desk and despite my attempts to shoo him away, he refused to budge. That's when it hit me that maybe this had been no chance encounter.

Henry quickly explained that *What Not to Wear* had become must see TV at the Jones' household and the twins thought it would be "awesome" if I were on the show. He made a few calls to a few friends he knew in television and long story short; the producers agreed with Henry that based on my appearance, I was a strong candidate. I had to take a week of work off to shoot the episode, much to the chagrin of Leighton who was bothered that I wasn't available to her.

Years later the rerun is still out there, even on airlines for the world to see. From the moment I was first stopped on the street bragging about my sense of fashion to the makeover and to my "new look". I felt like a movie star until of course I watched the episode, titled, *Hamper Girl.*

CHAPTER 30

Monday, March 13th, 2023
7:00 AM
From: The Desk of Liz White

As I was getting dressed in an outfit NOT chosen for me by the producers of *What Not to Wear*, it dawned on me that a long car ride would probably wrinkle my blouse, pants and jacket. So, I decided I would hang up my outfit in the car, and change once I arrived in Albany. I was also quite annoyed that it was Mike Rowe who was supposed to drive me. There was no fucking way I was doing that after his latest stunt, the Benedict Arnold that he was. I decided I would drive up with the family, the thought of which made me even more annoyed than I was already feeling. As I was applying makeup, very poorly I might add, my phone dinged, it was a text from Mike.

"Still riding up with me?"

I spent ten minutes putting together a text that would reflect how I was feeling about being betrayed, perhaps even used but as I was about to send it, I remembered that he's the media, the enemy, or certainly my enemy, so I changed my mind, and deleted the message. Instead, I wrote...

"Yes, let's get moving."

CHAPTER 31

March 13, 2023
8:00 AM
From: The Desk of Liz White

Mike Rowe arrived a half hour late outside my apartment building. Annoyed, I opened the rear door of his car and gently hung up my carefully chosen wardrobe. I also noticed the disgusting nature of his back seat. Fast food wrappers, empty bottles of soda and even beer bottles were littered everywhere.

"You're gross Mike," I said as I climbed into the passenger seat. "Ever think of cleaning your car?"

He tried explaining that he's in his car all day, thanks to his job as a field reporter, but I wasn't interested. Instead, I put in my earbuds.

"You're mad?"

I turned up the podcast I was listening to.

"Liz?"

"What?"

"My job is reporting the news, breaking news stories."

"It's gossip, not news, you're not a reporter."

Not a word was spoken for at least an hour, I knew this because I listened to my whole podcast, uninterrupted. Then Leighton called.

"Liz, where are you?"

"I'm on the road, we should be in Albany in ..."

"Good, listen, I don't know if you heard but Henry made the news for all the wrong reasons. I think we need to get in front of this so please check your email for a statement I just wrote and plan to release later today."

"A statement?"

Mike chimed in.

"What statement?"

"Never mind, it's none of your business."

"Liz, whom are you speaking with?" Leighton asked.

"Just the driver, Leighton. Nobody important," I said, making sure I made eye contact with Mike.

Leighton continued...

"Let me know what you think and get back to me. Time is of the essence!"

"Leighton, perhaps you should speak with an attorney first before saying anything? I suggested.

"Liz, I have a law degree, remember? WHY DO PEOPLE ALWAYS FORGET THIS???!!!" she shouted into the phone before hanging up.

True to her word, she did write a statement:

This has been a trying time for my family. I love Henry and stand behind him but if it turns out there were improprieties in regard to an affair with a former assistant of his, this, as a 21st century woman, I cannot tolerate. Women today are strong, we are leaders and we must not fall victim to any man, whether he's our husband, father, etc. I am a role model for my two girls so I will withhold judgment for now but as I said, no man shall abuse any woman under my watch. Thank You."

I responded quickly by deleting the statement from her sent emails. It was gone forever; I was hoping she'd forget she even wrote it.

CHAPTER 32

Monday, March 13, 2023
12:00 PM
From: The Desk of Liz White

Mike and I arrived at the New York State Executive Mansion. As I retrieved my outfit from the backseat, again I found myself horrified.

Mike apologized, telling me about a recent problem with ants in his car due to all the trash and debris and he was embarrassed.

"Ants? What the hell is wrong with you?" I sneered.

Mike had his press ID but I had nothing so I waited until I too received clearance. Leighton, Henry and the girls were already there. I found a bathroom and quickly threw on my outfit. Feeling like a million dollars, I strolled through the Executive Mansion until Leighton took me aside.

"I've decided not to make a statement after all. It was brought to my attention that we should speak to a lawyer first."

"Yes, that was me who gave you that advice, Leighton."

"No, I don't think so." she said walking off to join the twins who were looking even more bored than usual.

As we waited inside what I guess you might call a holding area, I peeked outside to the garden where the announcement was to take place and it was packed with reporters. I wondered how many were on hand for the announcement vs. how many were on hand for Leighton, and I guess Henry too.

I decided to check up on the emails, not only mine but Leighton's. As I scanned her emails, I could see that Leighton and Henry were having a rather contentious back and forth argument.

Leighton to Henry: I don't understand this thing with Andrea. Who else knew? Did Liz???

Henry to Leighton: Liz knows, but I don't want to discuss it.

Leighton to Henry: I can't believe she'd keep something like that from me.

Henry to Leighton: I asked her not to discuss it with anyone. This is not my finest moment. LOL

There were more emails, this exchange was focused on the plane crash.

Henry to Leighton: I still deserve to know why you were flying secretly. How embarrassing for you!

Leighton to Henry: I'm not embarrassed.

Henry to Leighton: Did Liz know??

Leighton to Henry: Yes, she had my itinerary.

There was no itinerary.

CHAPTER 33

Monday, March 13, 2023
1:00 PM
From: The Desk of Liz White

I decided to watch the announcement upstairs on a TV in the residential quarters. The festivities kicked off with Simon at the podium flanked by Leighton and Henry with the girls standing dolefully behind their grandfather. Simon didn't waste time. He attacked Republican leadership and criticized the direction in which the GOP was taking the nation, perhaps the easiest way to get good press in liberal New York. He also promised transparency, better judgment and honest government. Most of what he said went ignored but when he took questions from the press, the fireworks erupted.

Inside Edition asked the first question.

"So, Governor Miller, tell us about your daughter, Leighton Jones. What are your thoughts on the crash and her mysterious disappearance?"

"That's not what today is about. I'm just glad everyone is ok and as you can see, my daughter Leighton, her husband Henry and my two amazing granddaughters, Jackie and Michelle, are with me. I count my blessings."

FOX NEWS was next.

"Your approval ratings are up since Leighton's name was leaked. Care to explain?"

"I think, I think, well, Leighton Jones, my daughter and her husband, Henry, I love 'em both."

Governor Miller was getting choked up.

CNN followed.

"Is it true, Governor, that Leighton Jones, married mother of two was secretly seeing her longtime lover? Does this bother you?"

"I love my daughter, she ..."

His voice trailed off; he was looking defeated as the press kept shouting questions. With her dad looking like a deer in the headlights, I looked at Leighton and I actually saw compassion for her father as he struggled to protect her while keeping the press conference from turning into a zoo. I prayed (despite being an atheist) that she might step up. Leighton needed to be honest but what were the chances of that?

Finally, tapping her dad's shoulder, Leighton literally stepped up to the mic.

"Ok, fire away!" she said confidently enough.

Mike Rowe took the lead but as he was speaking, I noticed an ant crawling on my neck, then another, then a third. Panicked, I remembered his filthy fucking car and his ant story! Fuck, shit! There were more ants, I was covered in them. I took off my jacket but there were even more on my shirt! As I was having my personal crisis, from the TV I heard Mike ask...

"Leighton, were you on the airplane that crashed last week in New Jersey?"

"Obviously. Next question." Leighton said smiling.

Mike wanted more.

"Why were you on that plane, Leighton?"

"To get to Philadelphia for a Philly cheesesteak, wit!. I've heard Pat's is the place to go!"

She had all the reporters laughing at that one, especially by adding "wit," meaning with onions. How Leighton knew that vernacular, I cannot say.

Mike persisted with his line of questioning as I desperately did my best to shake off the ant colony that had made my most expensive, best-looking outfit their new home.

"Leighton, are you in a relationship with Christopher Crimi?"

Leighton laughed.

"I was a young woman who for 24 years made every effort to do what was right. Good grades, a good college, and then like my father before me, I went to law school. After graduating I was stressed and I needed a break so Dad here told me to take one year off and plan a great adventure for myself. I did, I went to Italy to learn to cook. I met Chris, we were classmates and became friends for life. I'm so proud of him, but sorry to burst the bubble, he and I are just that, friends."

Questions from other reporters started with rapid fire as I studied the mirror to make sure more ants weren't still crawling around on my neck, head or hair.

"Leighton, why did you run from the crash? Why try and hide?"

I listened in as Leighton, that self-centered, self-loathing, selfish, distant, dislikable, abhorrent, egomaniac was being bombarded with questions from the New York media and holding her own but now, there she was stumped and cornered.

"Leighton, I repeat, why did you run from the crash?"

After giving it some thought, she finally answered.

"Who wouldn't run from a plane crash?"

Again, the reporters broke out in laughter. Even the governor was smiling as he took back control of the podium.

"Thank you, Leighton, Thank you America. See you at the polls!"

As Governor Miller stepped away from the podium and was ushered away by his handlers, questions were being lobbed at Henry this time.

"Henry, care to comment on claims your assistant's husband has been making about sexual improprieties?"

Shouting over the noise, in a less than impressive manner, Henry who seemed a little confused by the abrupt end to the press conference responded...

"Andrea Amadola was a fabulous assistant. She was the best assistant I ever had. Thank You."

As I stood there in just a bra and my dress pants, with ant bites up and down my arms and chest, there was Henry, telling the world that Andrea, not Liz, was the best assistant he ever had.

CHAPTER 34

Monday, March 13, 2023
2:30 PM
From: The Desk of Liz White

It was one thing to belittle me privately or even in front of the staff, but did Henry really feel it was necessary to share it with the media? Was there not something else he could have said like "no comment" or "Andrea was replaced many years ago by the very dedicated and talented Liz White!" No, instead, he gave them my head on a platter, not that anyone would notice, but that's how it felt to me.

I was with the family in the living room. As usual, the girls were bored and wanted to be driven back to school. I was attempting to figure out how to make that happen when Leighton took me aside.

"Liz, your blouse is a complete mess, it's not even buttoned correctly. Did you get dressed in the dark again?"

"Wardrobe malfunction," was all I could think of to say.

Thankfully, Leighton changed the subject.

"Do you think they bought it?"

"Bought what, Leighton?"

"My excuse for being with Christopher."

"It wasn't really an excuse, it was a fact, right?"

"I guess." She said suppressing a slight smile.

I knew Leighton so badly wanted to say more, to finally spill her guts so I pressed on.

"Leighton, When the plane crashed, why did you run off, why not wait for help?"

"I must have bumped my head."

Again, she reverted to stonewalling so again I tried hammering away.

"Leighton. Why did you have the taxi driver take you to the train station, why not straight back to Manhattan?"

"Oh, that. He was smoking, can you believe that, smoking in a car with a passenger. I thought about reporting him."

All I could do was shake my head as Leighton started to walk away but then quickly, she turned back in my direction.

"Oh, Liz, regarding Andrea, she was so annoying. You my dear, are by far our best assistant. I mean that."

"Thank you, Leighton. That's the nicest thing you've ever said to me." I answered in stunned disbelief.

"You're welcome, now do me a favor and figure out how to get rid of the twins. I've seen and heard enough from them."

"Working on it."

Henry and Simon approached us. Leighton looked at her husband.

"Go ahead, Henry."

"Liz, my apologies, you are every bit as good as Andrea was at her job, even better! I don't know why I said that."

Leighton complimenting me and Henry actually apologizing, two firsts all in a matter of seconds. As the four of us stood in a circle, Leighton continued,

"You see, Henry, I told you, Liz was the right candidate."

"Right candidate?" I asked.

"Yes, Henry, do you remember her name? I don't, well, anyway, Henry had met with this girl, she interviewed on 9/11. Henry had to walk down the stairs because the building was being evacuated. Anyway, he said she was a chatterbox. She drove him nuts, I often remind him, it's lucky he found you instead.

Henry agreed before adding,

"She was frumpy too."

Aired March 13, 2023 - 3:00 PM ET

THIS IS A RUSH RADIO TRANSCRIPT. THIS COPY MAY NOT BE IN ITS FINAL FORM AND MAY BE UPDATED.

[15:00:00]

BOB LEMOULLEC: 1010 WINS NEWS ANCHOR: You're listening to 1010 WINS NEWS. All news, all the time, I'm Bob LeMoullec, and here's what's happening. It's not often when three breaking news stories join forces and become one. That's exactly what happened this morning at the Executive Mansion in Albany. As Governor Simon Miller announced his bid to become the next President of the United States, he was surrounded by family, including his daughter, Leighton Jones, who was recently identified as the missing woman who fled the crash of a small plane in New Jersey, piloted by The Italian Plate founder, Christopher Crimi. Ms. Jones was standing to the governor's left at the press conference, to his right was his son-in-law, investment banker, Henry Jones, recently accused of carrying on a sordid affair with a former assistant. 1010 WINS reporter, Mike Rowe attended the press conference and has this report.

MIKE ROWE: 1010 WINS NEWS REPORTER: Thanks Bob, the fireworks were going off, as New York Governor Simon Miller attempted to keep the press conference's focus on himself, but it was his family the media wanted answers from, especially his daughter, Park Avenue Socialite, Leighton Jones, who finally explained her relationship with Christopher Crimi, the pilot and founder of The Italian Plate restaurant chain.

(SOUNTBITES)

LEIGHTON JONES: I met Chris, we were classmates and became friends for life. I'm so proud of him, but sorry to burst the bubble, he and I are just that, friends.

MIKE ROWE: 1010 WINS NEWS REPORTER: The Governor's daughter also attempted to clear up why she ran from the plane following the crash.

(SOUNDBITES)

LEIGHTON JONES: Who wouldn't run from a plane crash?" (Audience laughter)

MIKE ROWE: 1010 WINS NEWS REPORTER: Regarding her husband, Henry, recently accused by his former assistant's husband of an affair that involved rough sexual acts, Jones had this to say.

(SOUNDBITES)

HENRY JONES: Andrea Amadola was a fabulous assistant. The best assistant I ever had. Thank you.

MIKE ROWE: 1010 WINS NEWS REPORTER: So, there you go. Simon Miller wants to be the next President of the United States, Leighton Jones says running from a plane crash is an appropriate response and Henry Jones says the woman he's accused of having an affair with was a top-notch assistant. Reporting from Albany, I'm Mike Rowe, 1010 WINS NEWS!"

CHAPTER 35

Monday, March 13, 2023
3:30 PM
From: The Desk of Liz White

Just minutes after Leighton, Henry and I shared a very congenial yet insulting moment, Leighton was once again on my case for not being better prepared.

"Liz, so Richie is going to drive the twins back to school, you apparently have a ride with that disingenuous reporter, but Henry and I? How are we supposed to return to the city, by osmosis?"

Leighton had a point, in my angst to get everyone to Albany, myself included, I never considered the return route home. It was my idea to get rid of the girl's promptly as per Leighton's request so Richie made the most sense but that left the three of us in a bind. My first thought, and yes, it was an idiotic one, have Mike Rowe drive the three of us in his ant infested car, but that wasn't ever going to happen. If it did, that would be the end of my job for too many reasons to list. So, without a solution and Leighton and Henry both getting more frustrated by the second, I reached out to Governor Miller for help. He had an idea.

"It's improper but I understand the pickle that you're in so I'll have the chopper fly you guys back to the city. Just make sure you keep it quiet; the press would have a field day if they found out."

The Governor's helicopter was set to leave just as soon as the three of us were ready so Leighton and Henry said their good-byes while I stopped off in a bathroom to make a quick wardrobe change, wanting nothing more to do with my ant covered outfit. I returned to the living room but everyone was gone. Confused, I approached an aide to the governor who was in the kitchen reviewing some paperwork.

"You're not flying home?" he asked.

"No, I am, I just wanted to change, where are Leighton and Henry?

Without looking up from his work he told me that as far as he knew they already left for the city. Stunned, I again started to explain that I too was supposed to be on the helicopter but I was met with a blank stare. Humiliated, I quietly slunk away.

I wanted to cry. This was as low a blow as I had ever dealt with. They just left me, no regard for my feelings or my well-being. Left, like I didn't matter. Without a clue as to how I was supposed to return to the city, I called Mike Rowe who quickly picked up.

"Liz? I figured you were done with me for good." He said sounding relieved that I wasn't.

I asked him if he still had room for one more and he laughed. He told me he was still on the grounds and to meet him by the car. I did, and of course he had a small vacuum in hand.

"These damn ants. I'm covered in them!" he admitted.

We didn't say much on the return trip to New York and I also decided not to tell him about what his ants did to me. We did listen to a repeat airing of his report made an hour earlier from the mansion, a report that included Henry telling the media that Andrea was the greatest assistant. Once back in the city, he stopped off in front of my apartment building. Feeling blue, but also horny, I invited Mike upstairs.

"Go find somewhere to park, I'll be waiting for you." I said leaning over to kiss him.

Mike thanked me for the offer but admitted he had a date so instead I got out of the car and as dramatically as I could, slammed the door. As I made my way back into my apartment, tired, rejected and itchy from ant bites, I showered, before applying a bottle's worth of Calamine lotion to my quickly developing scabs. I then went to bed knowing the man who was responsible for my ant bites was on a date.

CHAPTER 36

New York Post headline:

SHE WANTED A CHEESESTEAK!

There was high praise amongst the media and social media sect regarding Leighton's performance. She was called shrewd, charming and even hilarious. As far as her appearance, that too was applauded with one fashion critic even calling her a trend setter who could and I quote, "set the world ablaze with her stylings. From her now infamous Hermes Berkin bag to her Christian Louboutin shoes to her Valentino Garavani silk chiffon mini dress, Leighton Jones plays the part all too well."

As for Henry, he seemed to be in the clear too thanks to Andrea who stepped up to the plate in his defense. She stressed to a *New York Post* reporter that her soon to be ex-husband was full of shit and that Henry, who had been her employer, was a friend but they had never been romantically involved. She also admitted that Henry, bless his heart, kept her on the payroll, to the tune of $150,000 a year. That was about $20,000 more than I made. Not a bad chunk of change for someone's who sole responsibility was providing phone sex.

Despite the good news, I arrived later than usual for work, still furious about being forgotten in Albany. I assumed Henry would be steamed too about me not arriving on time but I was prepared to explode just as soon as he tried to bring up my tardiness. Instead, I was met with a smiling Henry who was as happy as I'd ever seen him, Andrea letting him off the hook obviously being a big reason.

"Liz, check this out!"

With his shirt sleeves rolled up on the ground in a pushup position and with one arm behind his back he started thrusting himself up and down on just the one hand. He did 10 of them as I stood and watched the spectacle. After completing them, out of breath, he explained,

"I couldn't sleep last night. *Rocky* was on, I think the third one."

"*Rocky III*" I said.

"Yes, Liz, obviously, so anyway, he was doing one armed pushups so I tried them too! Not bad for an old timer!"

I just nodded my head in resignation. The planned fight I wanted to have would have to wait thanks to Rocky Balboa so, instead I sat down at my desk and as if on cue, the phone rang, it was Leighton.

"Liz, I was surprised that you didn't come with us on the helicopter but I understand, that boytoy reporter friend of yours, I get it, you like him."

I wanted to shout into the phone, tell Leighton off for what had become of my life because of her, because of Henry, because of her stupid twins but instead, once again, I said nothing, I just scratched at my ant bites as Leighton continued ...

"Liz, my advice to you, journalists struggle to make a living. I'll repeat to you what my mother used to say, it's just as easy to marry a rich man as it is a poor man."

"Thank you Leighton, but I don't think Mike and I have much of a future together."

"Why, did something happen between the two of you?"

"Well, he did try and embarrass my bosses."

"Yes, this is true Liz, but he didn't. Anyway, changing the subject, the girls called. They say they're being punished for going AWOL? The school was not given notice that they would be away for a few days? They were even conversations about having Richie arrested for kidnapping? What is the meaning of this?"

Not once had it crossed my mind to alert the school that the twins would be out of town for a few days. Of course, one might think that responsibility would fall on a parent but no, instead I would be the fall guy. Exhausted, frustrated and ready to explode, I did just that.

"Leighton, I have been bending over backwards since the plane crash to get you everything you need. Everything Henry needs, everything, the twins, hair dresser appointments, flight reservations, cancel this, reschedule that. Food shopping! I even cleaned your bedroom Leighton!" I said louder than I meant to.

I was met with silence.

"Leighton? Leighton are you there?"

My other line rang. It was Leighton, her called had dropped meaning she likely missed some of what I had just said.

"Liz, so as I was saying, I explained the situation to the school so no worries but in the future, please remember, a parental note is needed anytime the girls leave campus. Also, I'm not sure if you saw the headlines this morning. I'm receiving more attention than I deserve but you know, I guess it's my 15 minutes! So, do me this favor, get a hold of let's say 50 copies of that wretched *New York Post*. You know what, make it 100. OK, got to pop. Ciao!"

Leighton hung up. She never did hear my temper tantrum.

As I rubbed my eyes, pondered it all and wondered what would be next, Henry snuck up on me, still panting from his late night movie inspired pushup regiment.

"Hey Liz, you know that whole thing about phone sex?"

"Yes, sadly I do."

"Well, it turns out I misspoke."

"Really?"

"Yep, I just wanted to clarify."

"Thanks Henry, noted."

"Ok then, you know what I could really use right now?"

"Phone sex?"

"Good one, Liz." Henry said with his patented frown. "No, what I could really use is one of your delicious cups of coffee."

CHAPTER 37

Tuesday, March 14, 2023
10:00 AM
From: The Desk of Liz White

An investigator from The National Transportation Safety Board called asking for Henry but, shockingly, I was told to take a message. Surprised, I attempted to explain why this was a bad idea.

"Henry, he's an important person and he needs to speak with you regarding the crash, maybe you'll actually learn more about the circumstances."

"Take a message" he repeated again, this time with authority.

I tried doing just that but the investigator, a Mr. Richard Marshall, was persistent.

"Mr. Marshall, perhaps I can help you." I said hoping that would satisfy his ire.

Frustrated, and wanting little to do with me, he left me his number but not before getting my name. After hanging up, I immediately googled any information on what happens if you refuse a request from the NTSB but there was nothing I could find. As a rule, people generally don't try and evade the National Transportation Safety Board.

CHAPTER 38

Tuesday, March 14, 2023
1:00 PM
From: The Desk of Liz White

I left the office early to help Bevy celebrate her 39th birthday. It had become a tradition between the two of us. Both being single, she would take me out for my birthday, and me for hers, always using Henry's credit card. As we sat together at a Korean barbecue joint not far from the townhouse, our conversations centered around Leighton, Henry and the NTSB.

"The investigator from the plane, he keep calling and even stop by but Mrs. J, she avoid him, always." Bevy said between bites of her chicken. "The man says there could be a fine. I tell, Mrs. J but she says fine is fine, better than talking about the crash."

I told her I was dealing with the same weird bullshit on my end at the office with Henry too. Bevy laughed.

"Those two, *liliac rahat nebun*. That's what they are."

"What does that mean?"

"It's Romanian, it mean, Mr. and Mrs. J, bat shit crazy!"

Bevy had a point. We weren't sure what Leighton was trying to hide but Henry seemed to be following her lead. What could this be about? We were both bewildered.

Changing the subject, Bevy asked if I knew of an actor named Matt Dyson. I did, I was a huge fan of his back when I was a little kid and he was a member of the famed 1980's brat pack along with Tom Cruise, Emilio Estevez and C. Thomas Howell to name a few. Since then, he remained a successful actor, maybe not an Oscar winning type of actor, but a working actor and still drop dead gorgeous.

"Of course, why?" I asked.

"He ask me out."

"What?? He asked you out? You're kidding, when?"

"Today."

"What? Matt Dyson?"

I was trying not to sound incredulous but this just didn't sound right. Bevy wasn't unattractive, but she certainly wasn't Hollywood. Heck, she was a cook and a maid from Romania.

"Yes, he was very nice. He see me at Citarella Market last week. People kept asking to take a picture with him so I knew he was famous. He wanted to talk to me. We went for coffee. He think it's funny I'm Romanian. He wanted to know about Transylvania."

Bevy's connection to Transylvania was always a topic, especially with Henry who kept his distance, claiming he did so just in case she was a vampire. I asked Bevy for more details.

"I fuck Matt's brains out!" Bevy said smiling.

"You did what?!" I asked nearly spitting out my meal.

Bevy laughed.

"No, we kiss a little after he took me for coffee. He got my number and called me this morning to wish me happy birthday and ask me to dinner!"

I didn't know if I should laugh or cry. Why wasn't that me? I was the one with his poster on my wall growing up. Bevy never heard of him but she was the one dating him? My life was getting more pathetic by the minute.

"Did you tell Leighton about Matt?" I asked.

"I did, she tell me, he a good catch and rich. She like that."

"Well, Bevy, I guess it's just as easy to marry a rich man as it is a poor man."

Bevy looked at me funny.

"I don't understand what you mean, Liz."

CHAPTER 39

Wednesday, March 15, 2023

9:00 AM

From: The Desk of Liz White

Governor Miller called from Iowa where he was campaigning. He was irate.

"Liz, I have been reaching out to Leighton but so far, no returned call. Is there a problem I should be made aware of?"

"None that I know, Governor."

"Liz, this is important. It's been leaked that the NTSB has been unsuccessful in making contact with Leighton and it's just plain idiotic. Please, I need your help."

I looked in on Henry who was staring out his window overlooking Manhattan, seemingly doing nothing.

"Governor, Henry is here. Please, help me too. The NTSB is calling us as well and Henry is also refusing to speak with them. I don't know why."

"Liz, put him on."

I knocked on Henry's closed door before entering.

"It's Governor Miller and he's furious Henry. You need to take the call."

"What does he want?" Henry asked, in a rather not so interested tone.

"He wants you."

Sheepishly, Henry picked up the line. For a brief second, I thought about spying from the other phone but I decided against it. A presidential candidate discussing an NTSB investigation, I just felt like that was one mountain I didn't need to climb.

As Henry and the governor spoke, Richie called. He was in a bad mood. The threat of being arrested really angered him to the point where he was talking about quitting. He was also pissed off about Leighton making friends with her Florida driver, Ernie.

"Mrs. J, she runs down to Florida, meets a fucking driver, and becomes tennis buddies with the guy. Me? I play tennis. How come she never asked me to play? I like tennis."

I laughed, thinking Richie was joking but he wasn't.

"I'm done, this is it. The kids, they pick on me, Mrs. J, she takes advantage of me. Mr. J, he couldn't pick me out of a police lineup unless it was the back of my head and you, you're always looking down your nose at me too."

I was feeling bad for Richie because it was all likely true until he threw me into the mix.

"Looking down my nose at you? That is not true Richie."

"Yes, it is. Well, let Mr. J know I'm giving my two weeks. I'm done."

Stunned, I tried talking some sense into him.

"Richie, you can't just quit. How will you survive without a job?"

Richie went on the explain that he didn't need to work. His kids were grownup, his wife was a tenured history professor at Fordham University, something I embarrassingly didn't know.

"Richie, I had no idea you were set." I admitted.

"Two weeks and I'm done."

Richie hung up.

I quickly called Bevy, she had a good relationship with Richie so I was hoping she could knock some sense into him but Bevy wasn't interested.

"Liz, I think I may quit too! I saw Matt last night. He serious, he says he wants me in California when he act in new movie. He offering to pay for everything!"

I was living a nightmare.

"Bevy, please tell me you're joking."

"Liz, is it better for me to clean toilets? Why are you so disappointed?"

I wasn't disappointed, I was jealous.

CHAPTER 40

Friday, March 17, 2023
9:30 AM
From: The Desk of Liz White

As per Henry, the meeting was setup in the office conference room. Attending would be two officials from the NTSB, Henry, Leighton, Governor Miller and two lawyers hired by Henry. The atmosphere leading up to the sit-down was unlike anything I had ever experienced. For starters, I was being kept in the dark, but why was Henry involved? He wasn't on the plane. For that matter, why was the governor involved? He wasn't on the plane either. It was all so strange. And finally, why lawyers?

I had plenty of croissants from Aux Merveilleux de Fred and coffee on hand. I also spent time sprucing up the office. For some reason, I felt I needed to impress Leighton who rarely dropped in on us. The investigators, including Mr. Marshall, arrived first. Henry who was in his office acting as if he were busy when I knew he wasn't had me escort the men into the conference room. Soon after, the lawyers and the governor arrived too. Everyone was there except for Leighton.

The plan was to kick off the interview at 10:00 AM, but at 10:15, still no Leighton. Henry who didn't seem bothered was still relaxing in his office as the governor and the lawyers along with the NTSB investigators ate and drank coffee in the conference room. The presence of Governor Miller was certainly easing the tension as he held court, doing his politician thing.

As I sat at my desk, sweating, beginning to believe that Leighton was planning on being a no show, I received an alert from her Visa card to the tune of $66,000 paid to Ronnie Eisler, a San Francisco jewelry designer who Leighton made occasional very high-priced purchases from. Confused, I called Leighton to investigate. Surprisingly, she picked right up.

"Leighton, what's this I'm seeing about a charge from Ronnie Eisler?"

"Oh yes, it should be arriving today, it's being shipped to your home in New Jersey."

Leighton, again, had me confused.

"My home in New Jersey?" I asked not sure what she meant since it had been nearly 5 years since I left Hoboken and moved into the city.

"It was Ronnie's idea, to save on the taxes."

"Leighton, I don't live in New Jersey anymore. Was he planning to ship it to my old address?" I asked alarmed.

"Umm, well, this is a problem, Liz. When were you planning on telling me you moved?"

LEIGHTON! I MOVED YEARS AGO!" I shouted into the phone causing Henry to bolt from his office and Governor Miller from the conference room simultaneously.

As both of them stood directly in front of me trying to figure out what the situation was, I shifted tones and quietly asked Leighton where she was.

"I'm on the elevator. I should be there in a nano second, Liz."

"She's on her way up now. Should be just a minute." I said to Henry and a relieved Governor Miller. As they joined the NTSB investigators, I quietly asked Leighton if she had a tracking number.

"I'm not sure what that is, Liz."

The door to the office swung open and in walked Leighton still on the phone with me. She blew me a kiss as if I were a fan watching her red-carpet arrival, saw the men waiting for her inside the conference room and made her way there. I followed asking her if she wanted coffee.

"Of course not." was all she said as if not drinking coffee was the norm at a meeting.

I closed the conference door behind me and quickly looked up Ronnie Eisler's number in San Francisco and, despite it being quite early on the West Coast, I called his cell and lucky for me he answered though he was obviously groggy. I explained who I was and I why I was calling. Without delay, he got me the tracking number but he also told me that he had shipped the jewelry yesterday and it was due to arrive this morning, in New Jersey, to a building I no longer had anything to do with, under a name that wasn't mine.

After hanging up, I quietly entered the conference room where the proceedings were just getting underway. With Leighton sitting at the head of the table, the two investigators to her left, the governor directly across from her and the lawyers and Henry to her right, I whispered into Leighton's ear.

"The package from Ronnie Eisler is set to arrive later today in New Jersey. I need to leave right now to get it before it disappears."

"That's wonderful Liz! I'll call you if we need anything from you." She said dismissing me as if this was her office and I were her personal assistant.

Henry looked on confused but I had no time to explain so I threw on my jacket, and left the office, hoping to intercept the $66,000 package as quickly as possible.

Downstairs, I found Richie parked in front.

"Richie! I need you to drive me to Hoboken!" I shouted into the passenger's side window nearly giving him a heart attack.

"Liz, I can't. Mrs. J told me to stay right here. I'm not budging. By the way, did you give Mr. J my two weeks?"

"No, Richie, that's your job, quit if you must but I'm not involved. So, you won't drive me?"

"Nope, Anyway, what's in Hoboken?"

I was about to explain but decided against it partially due to Richie's infamous big mouth so instead, I hailed a passing taxi. It was unusually humid for March and the driver had the windows down which unfortunately did little to mask the musky, rather unpleasant smell. On top of that, the driver was annoyed that he had to make a trip to New Jersey so before he could whine even more, I tossed him a $20.00 dollar bill. That did the trick, nothing more was said as we crawled through the midtown traffic towards the Lincoln Tunnel.

Meanwhile, according to the tracking information, the package was on a truck set to be delivered this morning to my former address. My worries were threefold. Would the doorman sign for a package being delivered to a Leighton Jones, a woman who never lived there? If so, would he willingly hand the package over to me, considering that I no longer lived there and since my name wasn't Leighton Jones, would that be an issue too?

The lunacy of my life was playing out right in front of me. With the NTSB and the governor of New York sitting in my office, I was in a beat-up taxi, sweating on my way to New Jersey.

"What could be worse?" I said out loud to no one.

Then, my phone rang, it was Mike Rowe.

"Hi, Liz, look, I feel bad about how we left things off."

"So, I guess, your date didn't work out." I said rather smugly.

"No, she's not my type." Mike admitted.

"Oh, so I guess, I'm your type." I said hoping I wasn't setting myself up for another zinger. Instead, Mike flattered me.

"Liz, I think you're awesome. I mean that."

That made my day but I wasn't ready to let the reporter get over on me just yet.

"So, with the Leighton stuff over, you'll have to find a new story."

"Yes, and no." was all he said.

"Yes, and no?" What the hell does that mean?

"The NTSB is frustrated. The pilot is back in Italy and not speaking so it's going to have to be Leighton or bust. That should be interesting."

I laughed to myself. Here I was with a giant-sized lead since Leighton was actually speaking with investigators at that very moment but instead, I said nothing, proud of myself for protecting my bosses once again from the press.

We made some small talk which was fine by me since I was stuck in the taxi which included Mike nervously asking me out. Against my better judgment I agreed letting him know I was up for anything just as long as it didn't include his filthy, disgusting car. After hanging up and with the filthy, disgusting taxi still moving at a snail's pace, I decided to google Mike Rowe, curious to see what the world wide web had to say about him. He actually had his own Wikipedia page. He was born in New Jersey to public school teachers. Before landing in New York, he had been a radio reporter in Pittsburgh. He was divorced but had no children. There was also web-based celebrity site that focused on net worth. His was listed at $100,000. I looked up Matt Dyson next. His net worth? $17 Million dollars.

CHAPTER 41

Friday, March 17, 2023
12:30 PM
From: The Desk of Liz White

I arrived at my old building in Hoboken. According to the tracking information, the package had been signed for a half an hour earlier. I approached the doorman who I remembered from my days living there. Unfortunately, he didn't remember me. I explained the whole situation to him which seemed to bore him to no end.

"I signed for the package before seeing the name. Leighton Jones? Isn't that the woman from the plane crash?" he finally asked.

I again over explained everything. Leighton had the package shipped from San Francisco, but accidently had it sent to my old address, and that I was her assistant, and that it was really important that I retrieve the package and get it back to her ASAP. Still, he was skeptical.

"How do I know this isn't a scam?" he asked. How do I know the package wasn't meant for the current tenant?"

I begged him to call the shipper. He agreed but he was taking his damn time, helping others in need of his assistance first. Finally, he retrieved the package from the building's holding area. I was initially surprised at its size, much smaller than one might expect from a shipment worth some $66,000. As he dialed the number in order to speak with Ronnie Eisler, he was interrupted by a maintenance man who was covered in gunk. The two started to argue, causing the doorman to not only put his phone down but the package too. As they continued to bicker, I made a split-second decision, I grabbed the goods and made a run for it.

As I hustled away from the scene of the crime, not sure of where I was going, I turned back expecting to see someone chasing me but there was no one. Still, despite wearing uncomfortable shoes, I didn't slow down until I felt I was in the clear. I then called an Uber, sitting on the front steps of a four story walk up, trying to look as casual as I could, while waiting and praying that the car would find me before the police did.

CHAPTER 42

Friday, March 17, 2023
1:15 PM
From: The Desk of Liz White

From the back of the Uber, I opened the package just to make sure it was what it was supposed to be. It was, one necklace and two bracelets. I wasn't impressed with the jewelry, especially at that price. As we passed back into Manhattan, I noticed all the tunnel police which naturally made me nervous considering I was likely a wanted woman back in New Jersey. It did concern me that since I was crossing states lines my crime was now one of a federal nature. Safely back in Manhattan, I was beginning to calm down when Leighton called.

"Liz, where are you?"

"Leighton, I'm in an Uber, I have your package."

"Good, this think just wrapped up. I'll be back at the townhouse. Meet me there and please, don't tell Henry a thing. This can be our little secret."

Our little secret? The things I had done for Leighton now including grand theft. It took forever, but finally I arrived at the townhouse. Richie's empty car was parked out front meaning Leighton was home and Richie too was likely inside.

I was met by a crying Bevy. She was clearly distraught; I could only imagine what Leighton said to cause this. She asked if she could speak with me privately so we went to the "secret garden" as Bevy called it which was located just off the family kitchen. Despite its beauty, thanks to year-round planting and gardening by an award-winning horticulturalist, it was largely ignored by both Leighton and Henry meaning it was a good place for us to speak discreetly.

I assumed Bevy was about to go off on Leighton but instead she started to bawl.

"Matt, he just breakup with me. No more California."

I can't say this shocked me. Matt Dyson was after all a famous actor but that wasn't what Bevy needed to hear.

I explained that she shouldn't be devastated but instead be proud that she turned the head of a huge celebrity. I asked her what specifically led to the change of plans on his part.

"He says he thought I was younger. He says I'm old."

For the record, Bevy was 3 years younger than me.

As we chatted and Bevy began to calm down, we heard a moaning sound coming from around the corner of the garden behind two large potted River Birch trees. Bevy whispered.

"I think someone having sex."

Bevy was right, the unmistakable sound of a woman having orgasmic pleasure. Standing in complete silence, we continued to listen for the occasional moan. Finally, I pointed to the kitchen indicating that we quietly leave before getting caught, ironically me thinking that we were the ones doing something that could embarrass us.

Back inside, Bevy and I tried to figure out what the heck was going on. I told her that I saw Richie's car parked outside without him.

"Richie? He go to garden to relax sometime. He bring woman this time?"

I couldn't imagine even Richie being so brazen but he was threatening to quit. Was this his way of going out with a bang? I really found it hard to believe. Plus, he was married but I guess anything was possible. Whoever it was, we soon found ourselves laughing, a complete 180 from just moments ago when Bevy was crying.

"What's so funny?" Richie asked stepping out of the bathroom with a copy of the New York Post, the one with Leighton on the front page under his arm.

"Richie?" was all I could say.

"What?" Richie asked looking down at his fly. "I piss on myself?" What the fuck is going on?"

We quickly filled him in about the sex sounds coming from the garden. Now concerned, the three of us stepped outside to investigate. The moaning wasn't sex though, it was actually Leighton who somehow had fallen and nearly knocked herself out. She was sitting up with a little blood on her forehead.

"Oh shit!" Richie yelled before lifting her up and carrying her back inside.

"I feel stupid now, Liz." Bevy said to me.

"I do too. We can never tell anybody this, not ever!" I stated boldly.

"Too late, Richie the big mouth, he know." Bevy reminded me.

CHAPTER 43

Friday, March 17, 2023
3:00 PM
From: The Desk of Liz White

Bevy said it was the first time she had ever seen Leighton using the garden which explains how she fell over a planter before hitting her head on a bench. But why was she out there?

I called my contact at New York-Presbyterian Hospital who quickly set up an appointment with a neurologist, but Leighton refused to go, so I called Henry.

"Well, if Leighton says no, then it's no, I guess." He said abruptly.

I reminded Henry that she could have a concussion but he didn't seem alarmed.

"She'll be fine. She did just survive a plane crash, don't forget."

He had a point. Not a scratch falling from 10,000 feet above the earth but a trip to her garden, that nearly killed her. Despite me warning Leighton not to sleep after suffering a head injury, she decided to take a nap anyway. While asleep, I spied on her phone. Sure enough, her last call was to Christopher Crimi. I assumed she was filling him in on the NTSB and wanted to do so in the privacy of the seldom used garden.

Henry arrived back at the townhouse. I kept the phone call a secret but asked him how things went with the investigators. Henry admitted he didn't know.

"Leighton asked us to leave the room. It was just her and the investigators so we ate more of those stale croissants you ordered."

"Thanks Henry, appreciated. Did the investigators say anything to you?"

"Just that, the investigation would be rather routine and they'd probably have their findings published in a few months."

"I have to ask, Henry, why were you and Leighton avoiding all this? Why were you avoiding the NTSB?"

"Liz, Happy wife, happy life."

CHAPTER 44

Monday, June 22, 2023
9:00 AM
From: The Desk of Liz White

Three Months later

I'd like to say that Simon Miller went on to become the next President of the United States. I'd like to say that he was so impressed with my abilities he took me with him to Washington where I served our great nation with honor and pride. I imagined myself all dolled up at the inauguration parties, my hair coiffed by Frederic. Perhaps, I'd even have a handsome Washington insider boyfriend by my side.

I would no longer have to deal with Leighton. Instead, she'd have to go through me each and every time she needed something from her father. Henry would tell friends that I, not Andrea, was in fact his greatest assistant ever. It all seemed possible, until the press conference.

Simon's performance was universally panned and within two months he would quietly, and without fanfare, drop out of the race. On the other hand, Leighton became a media darling. She was soon receiving requests for interviews and even an appearance on *The View*. Leighton declined them all.

"Liz, I don't seek attention, that's something that my father enjoys, me I'm just a regular gal, with a regular life."

Of course, her "regular life" was now taking place aboard the private jet Henry purchased following his wife's frustration from being recognized every time she wandered through an airport.

I've often replayed the events of that crazy two-week period. I've concluded that Leighton and Christopher were always just friends and that she flew with him on his plane because it was something exciting to do. No other explanation made sense. Regarding Leighton's last-minute trip to Florida, a day after the crash. If she had the opportunity to board a spaceship to Mars instead, Leighton would have boarded that. To Leighton, being "there" is almost certainly superior to being "here." Once there, you can reinvent, or defuse the situation, or just change your focus, especially with $150,000 of disposable cash on hand.

Richie did follow through on his threat to quit. During his exit interview with Henry, one in which he did not receive any type of severance package, he warned Henry that he planned to write a tell-all book. I do believe I have beaten Richie to the punch.

Bevy actually made amends with Matt Dyson and dated him a few more times. Leighton even invited him to the townhouse where the four of them shared a dinner that I worked my tail off to have fully catered. I was happy for Bevy but somehow, I felt as if she had surpassed me in the pecking order. However, once Matt stopped calling her, Bevy returned to her domestic responsibilities, much to my relief. I'm not saying I'm happy she got dumped but I was getting tired of Henry showing me all the photos the four of them had taken together during their grand dinner. I found the picture of Henry and Matt comparing biceps especially annoying.

What about Ernie, the limo driver turned tennis ringer? He was Leighton's distraction from Christopher who was Leighton's distraction from Henry. No one knew for sure what Leighton saw in Ernie because he performed terribly during the Piping Rock tournament. Apparently, her ability to spot new talent had slipped. Ernie was shipped back to Florida and we haven't been in touch since.

As for me, I'm still sitting at my desk on the 55th floor. I'm still highly overworked, underappreciated and underpaid. I'm still looking for that husband and I'm still fucking Mike Rowe, much to the chagrin of Henry.

"Liz, I'll be honest, your boyfriend turned our lives upside down over such a non-story."

"Henry, it was a plane crash involving two really wealthy people."

"I don't think it's news, I never did and I just want you to know, I will take your relationship with this reporter into consideration when I calculate your year-end bonus." Henry said smugly enough before adding…

"You know what I could use right now? A cup of your delicious coffee!"

As I made both of us a cup, on the TV, I saw that *TMZ* was reporting the rumor that Simon Miller was planning to retire from public life, rather than seek another term as governor.

"A day late and a dollar short, *TMZ*," I said to no one out loud.

That wasn't the big story though. They were talking about possible candidates to run in his place. At the top of their list, Simon Miller's very popular and very well-liked daughter, Leighton Jones.

"Henry, are you seeing this???!!!" I shouted across the office.

Henry and I watched dumbfounded.

"This is insane, right Henry? I mean, what the heck?"

"Well, you never know Liz. This is New York. We've elected Andrew Cuomo, there was Eliot Spitzer. Andrew Weiner, don't forget about his weiner pics!" Henry said proud of himself for being clever.

"Oh, and Liz, we once had a blind Governor too! Don't forget him."

"Yes, but Henry, we're talking Leighton!"

My phone rang, it was of course Leighton.

"Yes Leighton?"

"*TMZ* is reporting I may run for governor! Let's work on my press release."

"To let them know you're not running?"

"No, to tell them that I am!"

Aired August 22, 2023 - 9:00 AM ET

THIS IS A RUSH RADIO TRANSCRIPT. THIS COPY MAY NOT BE IN ITS FINAL FORM AND MAY BE UPDATED.

[9:00:00]

BOB LEMOULLEC: 1010 WINS NEWS ANCHOR: You're listening to 1010 WINS NEWS, all news all the time. Here's what's happening. The National Transportation Safety Board has released its final report regarding a small plane crash involving The Italian Plate Founder, Christopher Crimi. Also flying on that plane was Leighton Jones, the Park Avenue Socialite and current New York Gubernatorial front runner to replace her father, Governor Simon Miller who is retiring. 1010 WINS NEWS reporter, Mike Rowe has all the details.

MIKE ROWE: 1010 WINS NEWS REPORTER: Thanks Bob, well no one saw this one coming. According to NTSB investigators, the pilot, Christopher Crimi was flying the single engine Cessna Skyhawk back on March 9th when he had a seizure. Unconscious, and with the plane in a tailspin, it was Leighton Jones who, without any flight training, successfully crash landed the plane onto a ballfield not far from Linden Airport in New Jersey. Attempts to speak with the modest Ms. Jones about her heroics have been unsuccessful, up to this point, but I did manage to get a statement from her long-time secretary, Liz White.

(SOUNDBITE)

LIZ WHITE: What? Bull(bleep). I don't believe that. That's just stupid! What is wrong with you? Please, just go away!

MIKE ROWE: 1010 WINS NEWS REPORTER: Even Leighton Jones' assistant is finding the whole story hard to believe but according to the NTSB, it's all true. Reporting from Midtown Manhattan, I'm Mike Rowe, 1010 WINS NEWS!